About the Author

Malcolm Gerloch was born in 1939, in Hull, East Yorkshire. He was educated at Hymers College there, and subsequently at Imperial College in London where he spent six years working for his bachelor and first doctorate degrees. After two years in post-doctoral research in magnetochemistry and ligand-field theory at the University of Manchester, he was appointed lecturer before moving, the following year, to University College, London. After three years, he was appointed to a post as Assistant Director of Research in chemistry in the University of Cambridge. He was awarded the degree of Doctor of Science there in 1980 and promoted to Reader in Inorganic Chemistry in 1984. He retired in 1999 and is an Emeritus Fellow of Trinity Hall. He and his wife, Gwyneth, now live in Canberra, Australia where they enjoy many of the usual pleasures of what might have been expected to be a quiet life in retirement. At seventy-eight,

Malcolm began writing non-scientific books to add to his four technical books and over 120 research papers. He currently boasts some dozen children's books, together with a collection of short stories and a couple of autobiographical accounts of life before and after retirement; he has recently completed his first novel. Malcolm has two daughters, three grandsons and innumerable stray cats.

Arnold Forbutt Esquire

Malcolm Gerloch

Arnold Forbutt Esquire

Vanguard Press

VANGUARD PAPERBACK

© Copyright 2024
Malcolm Gerloch

The right of Malcolm Gerloch to be identified as author of
this work has been asserted by him in accordance with the
Copyright, Designs and Patents Act 1988.

All Rights Reserved

No reproduction, copy or transmission of this publication
may be made without written permission.
No paragraph of this publication may be reproduced,
copied or transmitted save with the written permission of the
publisher, or in accordance with the provisions
of the Copyright Act 1956 (as amended).

Any person who commits any unauthorised act in relation to
this publication may be liable to criminal
prosecution and civil claims for damages.

A CIP catalogue record for this title is
available from the British Library.

ISBN 978 1 80016 948

This is a work of fiction. Names, characters, businesses, places, events and
incidents are either the product of the author's imagination or used in a
fictitious manner. Any resemblance to actual persons, living or dead, or actual
events is purely coincidental.

Vanguard Press is an imprint of
Pegasus Elliot Mackenzie Publishers Ltd.
www.pegasuspublishers.com

First Published in 2024

Vanguard Press
Sheraton House Castle Park
Cambridge England

Printed & Bound in Great Britain

It is my duty, but also my pleasure, to record the advice and encouragement of Maria Altman, Elizabeth Hillhorst, Sue King and Edith Richie. As ever, my wife, Gwyneth has spent hours reading and rereading proofs and early versions of this tale. I thank them all.

1

Arnold Forbutt has a quite dreadful kind of word blindness. Somehow, he gets confused over names of people and things. Separately, that is. Some people. Some things. He doesn't always do it, Mrs Malaprop probably wouldn't accept him as a cousin, and nobody has ever been able to work out just when he will do it. It has even been suggested that he does it in his sleep, but we know of no way to test that proposition. We must also draw attention to the fact that some folk have that ability to see beyond the obvious, to pick up somehow, on those little signs which so many of us seem not to sense. Arnold Forbutt is one of those.

Don't get me wrong, Arnold is a nice chap, gets on with everyone as far as I know, but appears to possess a higher degree of self-confidence than us mere mortals. He can pick things up at a glance. Never fails. Faultlessly divines whether someone is honest or not, seems never to be fooled by all those con artists on the web. Either that, or he fails to tell anybody that he has been had; or maybe, just begins to believe it himself. Practice makes perfect, they say. I guess that includes self-deception. Take that time when he got an SMS asking him to confirm or not a payment of $1,200 by PayUpPal. That made him sit up, I can tell you. He was in his car at the time and had just pulled over to find out what the ping was all about.

'Please confirm PayUpPal payment of $1,200. Call 12345' or some such number, the message said. Arnold had made no purchase costing anything like that amount recently. Or ever, as a matter of fact. His car engine was still running as he called the number. He had expected it to take a while to be answered, just like all his other experiences with calling big corporations, but no, he got through immediately.

'I wondered about that straight away', Arnold said afterwards. Always quick to smell a rat, our Arnold.

There began then an unbelievably lengthy rigmarole from the guy who answered, along the lines of, "For the purposes of security and best practice, may I inform you that this conversation is being recorded," and "For the purposes of security and best practice, may I have your full name?"

'Well, okay,' thought Arnold, 'It's good to be secure while discussing money matters.'

'Arnold Herbert Forbutt,' he replied, and added, 'How do I know you really are PayUpPal?'

Straight to it, see? 'Good to be careful,' Arnold said later.

The conversation moved onto statements like, "We will never ask you about your personal details over the phone, sir," and "We will not ask you for the number on your credit card."

'That was interesting,' Arnold remarked later, 'for I regularly give out that number to sellers of one kind or another.'

It's all a matter of trust, Arnold.

"For the purposes of security and best practice," the man from PayUpPal droned on, "could you confirm that the last four digits of your credit card are 6789?"

By the way, for purposes of security and best practice, I have invented these numbers. One cannot be too careful. Mind you, I don't actually know the right ones anyway.

"For the purposes of security and best practice, sir, could you tell us the name of the bank issuing your credit card?"

'Er, Bardlums, I think,' replied Arnold, realising that he did not have the card on him or, for that matter, any other documents, because ever since he had learned to pay for things by clicking his smartphone, he had stopped carrying documents. Actually, he was quite proud of having learned how to do that. He really felt that he was keeping up with modern society.

"I don't think that's right," replied the man on the phone.

'I remember that he had given me his name right at the beginning but, as usual, it had gone in one ear and out of the other,' Arnold recalled.

'No, no. You are quite right. It's Cammers,' Arnold replied. "That's right, sir," the man replied.

Arnold was beginning to get a bit irritated. Why ask me if you knew already? he thought. Seems reasonable to me.

"For the sake of security and best practice, sir, could you confirm that the first four digits on your credit card are 1234?"

'Sounds right to me,' replied Arnold, 'I'm working from memory, though,' he added.

"And, for the sake of security and best practice, sir, could you please tell me the second four digits on your credit card?"

'No, I can't,' replied Arnold.

"Why not, sir? We need those numbers for the sake of security and best practice."

'Because' Arnold replied, 'I'm in my car without my card. I don't carry it these days.'

"For the sake of security and best practice, sir, could you give me the third set of four digits on your credit card?"

'I just told you, I don't have the card with me,' Arnold replied, irritably. "Just bear with me, sir," replied the man on the other end of the line, 'while I consult with my colleagues."

That short pause gave Arnold the time to think about what was happening and for his doubts to grow. 'Look, I'm on my way home,' he said, 'When I get there, I can look at my card and give you the information you want. Meanwhile, can you please stop that payment of $1,200?

Give me your number and I'll call you back as soon as I get home.'

"How long will that be, sir?" enquired the man on the phone. 'About a quarter of an hour,' Arnold replied.

"Trouble is you might get someone else in the office, sir." 'Who should I ask for?' Arnold asked.

'Just ask for James, sir. I'll wait for your call.'

'I guess he's still waiting', Arnold told us later, ''cos the first thing I did when I got home was to get onto PayUpPal via their website on my computer. They sounded quite different, never once mentioned security or best practice, told me that there was no record of any payment for $1,200 pending or executed and that I should just ignore the phone call. "We never contact you by phone," they said. 'I just knew that guy was fake right from the first sound of his voice,' Arnold triumphally concluded later.

Well, he always had had an ear for these things. I just guess it was lucky that he wasn't carrying his credit card with him. And, by the way, for the purpose of accuracy and protection from litigation, it should be pointed out that Arnold had this little tick: sharp as a tack though he was, he had this tendency to misremember names. He nearly got them right, though. But he does see through things. I've told you that already.

Arnold is like that, you know; but for Arnold, we might all end up in the soup. Perspicacious is the word, I think. I mean, take the other month. No, come to think about it, I think it was over eighteen months ago, now.

Anyway, he noticed a couple of cats circling each other in his and his lady-waife's back garden.

'Hey, Molly, look at that. Dost tha reckon yon's a good omen, luv?' Arnold and Molly often put on a quasi-Yorkshire accent when talking privately. It was part of their deep love for each other. Arnold has an ear for these things. The cats continued to circle for a bit until one of them spied Arnold and his better half eyeing them through the window. The cats eyed them back before gracefully – not at all hurriedly – retreating whence they had come.

'I miss having a cat, luv,' Arnold said.

'So do I, feyther,' she said, 'But it's no use. At our age, we cannot cope with having cats again.'

Arnold said nothing, for he agreed with that view. They had discussed it many times. He still fancied having one, though.

'I'm off to the shops,' he said.

Having retired many years ago and moved home from England to Australia, life now seemed to consist of shopping, cooking, eating, reading and watching the telly. When he got back and unpacked his groceries, he glanced out into the garden, something he often did, for he was also quite a keen gardener. Twenty metres from the house, he had laid a small area of crazy paving some years ago.

Look, it's not really important why that bit of crazy paving was there except insofar as it does illustrate the way Arnold thinks. Well, I think so. You see, several years ago, Arnold had suspended a triple planter comprising large, heavy terracotta dishes on three strong galvanised chains from an overhanging tree branch high above. He didn't actually plant anything in the three shallow dishes, however, for that would have involved his watering them regularly, remembering how hot it gets in Australia. He didn't mind the effort that would be involved but, he had reasoned, should he forget to do it for a couple of weeks, any plants would die, and plants are expensive. So, Arnold reasoned – for he was, indeed, a most reasoning sort of man – he wouldn't plant anything there at all. One might ask why he chose to place the planters there in the first place if he had no intention of using them as such and, in truth, Molly had asked that question. But the answer is lost in the haze of seniors' memory or was ignored; something like that. It so happened that, at around that time, a couple of cockatoos flew in to perch on these planter saucers. Sulphur-crested cockatoos are rather splendid birds. They are quite large, perhaps a third of a metre long, with lovely creamy-white feathers, black eyes with pronounced lids, or so it seems, and bright yellow combs on top of their heads. They fan out these combs when arguing – which they do quite often and make quite a racket when they do – or simply when landing, rather as if, by fanning out their combs, they balance out the sudden loss of momentum. They are quintessentially THE Australian bird. Their song, if that's what you want to call the sound of a 1920s Ford grating its gears, is quite appalling. And loud. Having said all that, however, it has to be said that they are most astounding-looking creatures. Anyway, Arnold decided that year to encourage the birds to visit his and Molly's garden. A regular visit to the supermarket yielded large bags of miscellaneous seed which Arnold tossed in handfuls onto the terracotta saucers. They were intended to be planters, remember, so they had sizeable holes in their bottoms for reasons of good drainage. So it was that a fair amount of the bird seed slipped through these holes and onto the ground. There was every hope, however, that the birds would spot these tailings and hoover them up. The birds soon found the offerings and passed the word. Arnold and Molly were delighted and intrigued to watch cockatoos – six or eight at a time, for goodness' sake – climbing down the galvanised chains to the large terracotta saucers. When they had consumed the contents of the top one, they climbed the foot or so down to the next one. It was hilarious to watch how they did this for it seemed that the easiest way for them to work around one dish so as to continue their downward climb towards the next, was to turn upside down as they negotiated the obstacle and then to right themselves once onto the next section of the chain.

Now please understand that cockatoos are very untidy eaters. They are clever enough to use their claws to pick up the seed and put it into their mouths – something that only adds to their charm in Arnold's view – but they do it so carelessly and with absolutely no regard for their hosts' tidy garden, spraying seed all over the place. Thing was that next spring their scattered seed took root and long grasses began to grow where pristine pebbles formerly defined the groundcover. Arnold was not happy.

'I'm not happy, luv,' he told Molly, as if it were her fault.

Arnold was nothing if not a thinker though. He thought it through. He decided to lay a small area of crazy paving under those planters.

'Seed 'll not grow on that', he told Molly. 'No dear,' she agreed.

He spent a fair amount of money buying the stone for the crazy paving and a great deal of effort digging in around the large roots of the large tree from which those planters were suspended so as to lay a good depth of concrete under the paving stones. He thought it through, for Arnold was nothing if not a thinker, and he realised full well that those tree roots would grow in time – even though the tree was already very large – and so he wrapped the roots in old carpet underfelt before putting down the concrete. The crazy paving looked very good, everyone agreed, even if it was a bit higher than one might have wanted – as an ideal, you might say.

One day, however, the cockatoos bit off the young shoots of Arnold's then favourite plants. Pieris, they were. Arnold, who is normally an easy-going sort of chap – well, he likes to think so, and maybe he's right – completely lost his rag. He shouted at the cockatoos and waved his arms angrily. The birds barely moved and looked back at him in amazement and, Arnold insisted, with some amusement. Possibly with derision. Arnold didn't see the joke one little bit.

'They *are* called flying secateurs, luv,' Molly carelessly remarked.

Some weeks later, Arnold explained all this rigmarole to their neighbour, Rob, who then remarked that he too was getting more than a little fed up with the cockatoos chewing off large bits of his decking. Cockatoos are wont to gobble wood. Rob gently pointed out that it was all Arnold's fault for encouraging the destructive birds.

'They're sometimes called flying secateurs,' he remarked.

Arnold said nothing. He had a sense about when to say nothing, did Arnold. 'Am I allowed to shoot them with an air pistol?' Arnold asked a third party one day.

'No, 'fraid not, but you could buy a water cannon.'

And so it came to pass that, holding a child's large water cannon, purchased from ToysRUs, Arnold chased the damn cockatoos from the garden. It took three separate attempts on three separate days, chasing the birds all over the place until, with a great deal of raucous yelling, those very loud birds surrendered and flew off for good. Actually, for the sake of accuracy and best practice, I must record that one bird comes back into the garden on an annual basis, obviously just to check if there's any seed in the planters. Cockatoos have very long memories. They find nothing and fly off for another year.

Where was I? Oh yes, I was explaining why there was a small arc of crazy paving in the middle distance from the back of the house. So now you know. After spending God knows how much on planters, then deciding not to use them as planters, then to use them as bird feeders costing a considerable sum in bird seed by the way, then laying crazy paving so as to prevent the seed spray from the untidy cockatoos taking root, then driving off the cockatoos after buying a complex water cannon … Oh, by the way, for the sake of completeness and best practice, I must record that more recently, the wind blew down the tree and smashed the planters, pulling up the crazy paving as it fell. Since then, half of that paving has been saved. It's all a story of the ravages of time and of the futility of man's efforts. Well, of Arnold's anyway.

So now, getting back to the main story about the day that Arnold and Molly first saw a couple of black or dark cats circling each other. Remember? Well, after Arnold returned from his shopping, and looked out at the garden, he saw a large dark object resting on that little patch of crazy paving.

'What on earth is that, luv?' he was about to say, when said object moved and he realised that it was simply a pair of cats copulating. A black cat was covering (such a posh word for it, don't you think?) a brindle-coloured cat. After a few moments, the black cat wandered off and the brindle-coloured female slowly sashayed towards the house, almost as if to say, 'Seen enough now?'

It was then that Arnold's quick mind came into play. But for Arnold Forbutt's sentimentality, the next three years of their lives might have been far simpler. He decided to leave out a small saucer of milk for the brindle-coloured cat for otherwise, he reasoned (did I mention that

Arnold was a good reasoner?), that the cat would struggle to survive as she moved towards motherhood. But for Arnold Forbutt, the cat might not be able to fend for herself.

That's why cats have been around for thousands of years.

Arnold placed the saucer fairly near the house but not on the deck immediately outside the back door which would have been more convenient for him and, by the way, was where he and Molly had fed another cat a couple of years earlier before it died. Anyway, he and Molly kept a close lookout to see if they had snared the beast which, incidentally and inventively, they decided to call Brindle.

Well, Brindle did come back, was extremely wary but, in due course, drank the milk. By degrees, and by adding bread and other solid cat food, Arnold managed to accustom Brindle to eating breakfast in the early morning and tea in the middle of the afternoon every day. A kind of silver service, you might say. Cat-food bills grew. Arnold tried opening the glazed, sliding door to the deck while Brindle was eating, or shortly afterwards, and saying a few friendly words to her in the hope of a purr or even a stoke. Brindle was having none of it. She was as skittish as they come and never stayed within six or more metres of the food bowl if The Man was around.

Of course, their neighbours, Gordon and Mavis Dunport pointed out that she was feral and a neighbourhood pest. Mavis did bring round a dish of salmon, nevertheless. Molly insisted, however, that

Brindle was not exactly feral. It was almost certain, she asserted, that she had belonged to some local family but had been abandoned. Apparently, there are people in this world who, on leaving a locale for whatever reason, simply abandon their children – er, cats. Arnold and Molly were appalled by the thought of so selfish and unfeeling an act, but it has since been confirmed that such things do happen. So Brindle was abandoned, rather than feral. Molly said so, and so it must be so.

As time passed, Brindle came to trust Arnold a little more, but progress came at a glacial pace. She no longer flew off as the door was slid open. Only as he put a foot outside. But Arnold persisted. He would talk to Brindle in soft tones as he lay her breakfast out on the deck and, as time went by, she didn't run away.

But nor did she come any closer. The weeks slipped by. Arnold had done a little reading and expected to see kittens after about eight weeks. Nothing. After about ten weeks, Brindle disappeared herself, not coming in for meals for a couple of weeks. 'So that's the end of that,' Molly and he supposed.

But no! eventually, Brindle reappeared, with two kittens in tow. One was a darker form of her own brindle colouring, the other, pure black, although Arnold did notice something of a reddish hue when the sun shone through its fur. It all seemed only too logical to Arnold, remembering that black cat which he had seen bonking Brindle on day one. For purposes of security and best practice, by the way, I must acknowledge that it was only

Day One from Arnold's point of view. Arnold would like such details made clear. Anyway, he popped out to his local supermarket and bought some packets of kitten food: nice jellified, sweet-smelling stuff, it was. A bit previous, though, you might say, for the kittens were not yet weaned and Brindle ate the whole packet herself.

'Still,' thought Arnold, 'she needs the sustenance to make her milk for her kids, so it wasn't wasted. It gets there in the end.'

Very knowledgeable, our Arnold.

Molly and Arnold cooed over their new children every day, observing in minute detail, every little sign of growth. They would have put their names down for Eton if it weren't at the other end of the Earth. And, of course, if they had names.

'What shall we call them?' asked Molly a few weeks later. 'Are they boys or girls?'

Without hesitation, Arnold identified the brindle-coloured kitten as male and the black one as female.

'How do you know?' asked his ever-loving.

'Just look at the brindle-coloured one's face,' he said. 'If ever there was a male face, that's it. No doubt about it.'

'Well,' thought Molly, 'Arnold does have an eye for these things.' 'We'll call him Brindleson,' Arnold exclaimed, feeling rather clever at finding an apt name so easily. Before retirement, back in England, they had a couple of Burmese cats. The present black kitten had the same sort of strong, slinky, lithe look of their former female brown Burmese cat and it could jump almost as effortlessly. Clearly female. You have to have an eye for these things, Arnold remarked.

'Let's call her Dark Eyes,' Molly suggested. It's correct to say that her eyes were darkish, but the truth is that Brindleson's eyes were even darker. But then, no naming system is perfect, after all.

Well, after all that effort, a cup of coffee was called for. Retirement can be a bit like that.

The weeks passed by, the kittens grew stronger, they were weaned now and were climbing all over the garden. It was a delight to the Forbutts to see these wriggling balls of fur hopping all over the place; making a spirea suddenly shake with laughter as one of their kids appeared from within. Arnold was less amused, however, when Dark Eyes suddenly climbed right to the top of his favourite gleditsia tree. Arnold had been carefully nurturing this tree for some years, for it had had a poor start after being transplanted from horticulturist pot to ill-prepared garden soil. But it had finally decided to make a go of it and to reward Arnold for his bumbling efforts. Trouble was, that its branches were still slender and could hardly bear the weight of so well-fed a kitten as Dark Eyes. Molly and Arnold had observed that Dark Eyes was growing at a fair old rate. More than Brindleson.

Arnold rushed outside. 'Off!' he yelled at the mountaineer. For purposes of security and best practice, maybe one should acknowledge that mountaineer is not the most apposite word for a tree climber: however... Dark Eyes had not heard so stern a rebuke before and jumped back down to Earth immediately. Arnold promptly relented. 'Good girl!' he said, more quietly, and all was forgiven. The fact that no branch of the Gleditsia had been broken undoubtedly contributed to this happy ending. There were excursions into the fig tree as well but don't for a moment imagine that Dark Eyes was after the fruit. Not a bit of it: she was after the birds that rummaged around in there, looking for any fruit which had been silly enough to ripen. Arnold saw this as something of a win-win situation and didn't interfere, for the fig tree was old enough and stout enough to look after itself.

Occasionally, none of the three cats came in for breakfast, and indeed such rejections of Arnold's munificence often occurred for perhaps three or four days in a row. In the beginning, Arnold and Molly were both somewhat deflated, thinking that these nominally feral cats (no, they weren't!) had gone off for good. But they returned and, in due course, Arnold would refer to these absences as Brindle taking her kittens "on manoeuvres". In other words, teaching them the ways of the wild. As far as Molly and Arnold were concerned, that was a bad thing because firstly, they couldn't bear the thought of their protégés gobbling mice, birds or any other living creature, and secondly, did not want their neighbours or the authorities in general branding them as feral and ripe for extermination. The cats, that is. Anyway, as I said, after absences of a few days, Brindle would bring her brood back home. Arnold and Molly were... ecstatic, I think the word is.

Apart from these occasional hiccoughs, life with the cats continued at a steady and contented pace. Until, that is, Brindle disappeared on her own for a couple or so days. Dark Eyes and Brindleson seemed unfazed and continued to grow and eat the Forbutts out of house and home. Until, that is, Brindleson also disappeared. Molly and Arnold were puzzled and somewhat concerned until Brindleson reappeared after a few days, trailing three kittens behind her. Arnold spotted them early on because, as we know only too well, he had an eye for these things.

'Well, I'm not going to change the name,' he announced, 'she can't tell the difference and any change might confuse her.' So there you have it.

Brindle, herself, returned after about ten more days. She brought four kittens with her. The fact that her kittens were a fair bit larger than Brindleson's suggested that Brindle had given birth first and had been attending them in their earliest days in private under a hedge somewhere. After a slow walk around the garden, Arnold reckoned her knew where. He has an eye for such things. It also seemed clear that Brindle and Brindleson had been mated by different cats, because while Brindleson had produced two ginger and one black kitten, Brindle was proud to display two ginger, one fair or fawn, and one pure white offspring.

Soon after returning with her brood, Brindle set about getting rid of Dark Eyes as the unwanted male cat around the place. Arnold spotted this more or less as soon as it happened, for he has an eye for these things. Molly and Arnold were very upset to see Brindle hissing Dark Eyes off the premisses and valiantly tried to thwart her efforts by providing an extra bowl of cat food at a somewhat later time and even, on one occasion, at the front door rather than the back. But it was all to no avail, for Dark Eyes had gotten the message clear as day. He had been told to bugger off and he did so. He was never seen again at the Forbutts' place. That brought considerable sadness but, in truth, it was ameliorated by the presence of the two new litters.

The cat count, in case you haven't been paying attention, was now nine. 'We're becoming a cat factory, feyther,' Molly observed, 'This can't go on. It's only a matter of time before one or more of this brood gets pregnant.' Arnold agreed, for he's not slow of thought.

Gordon, next door, complained that some of the kittens were using his vegetable patch as a toilet. 'I can smell it,' he said. His face very clearly showed that he could.

That's considerate of them to poo off-piste, thought Arnold but, wisely, said nothing except a rather tame, 'Sorry'. However, it was clear that Gordon was not happy, and Mavis pointed out, yet again, that these feral cats would just keep on reproducing. All of that was blindingly obvious to Arnold and Molly, and they really didn't want to upset their neighbours, who were also their friends, but they really didn't know what to do.

'Get onto the RSPCA,' Mavis insisted.

'Okay,' thought Molly, 'but I don't want them killed. They must be re- homed.' Arnold agreed.

Molly began to make overtures to the RSPCA. They immediately assured her that they would certainly not euthanise the cats and said that they'd send Len around in two days to set about catching the cats and taking them away. Arnold took Len around the garden, showing him where he thought Brindle had raised her brood and pointed under the house where it was now clear that all the cats stayed most of the time when not running, jumping and generally having fun and being ornamental in the garden.

Immediately Len caught sight of Brindleson, he said, 'She's a nice little girl.'

'How do you know it's a girl? Just like that?' asked Arnold. I mean, damn it, how come this yet-to-shave boy immediately and correctly identified Brindleson's sex, he wondered with some chagrin?

'Oh, that's easy,' Len replied, 'Brindle-coloured cats are always female.' That's a well-known fact in the trade, apparently. But not well-known to Arnold. 'That's not fair!' he blurted out. After all, using specialist knowledge, for goodness' sake... Len looked at him without understanding, and Arnold let it drop.

Len said that he would return with a cage in two days. He also explained that the RSPCA had a limited budget and it seemed to Molly and Arnold that feral cats came way down their list of priorities. This, despite their saying on Molly's first phone call to them that they were indeed aware of there being a feral cat problem in that area. As it happened, Molly and Arnold had come across these cages already because they had agreed to have one in their garden when some people from down the road had sent a note around the neighbourhood saying that their beloved cat, Dom, had gone missing. Arnold and Molly had often heard cats wailing outside their bedroom in the wee small hours and wondered whether one of those might be Dom. So, yes, they agreed to try and catch Dom for these bereft supplicants. They were successful immediately and managed to catch three different cats on three consecutive nights. None was Dom. The cats were not amused and made their feelings very clear. The Forbutts gave up after that. For the sake of completeness and best practice, by the way, I wish to record that Dom was found six months later in a suburb some eight kilometres away. He was returned to his owners and, as far as history records, was happy to be so and remained with them thereafter. Anyway, the Forbutts were somewhat wary of the use of these cages to catch their beloved cats but understood the necessity. Len suggested putting their grub into the cage without setting it so that the cats would get used to it and be easier to catch thereafter.

Well, he was right, for after only a couple of moments, several of the cats explored the inside of the cage before wolfing down their meal. All seemed set; except the trap, that is. Several days later, Len returned to set the contraption, something which neither Molly nor Arnold felt like doing. Somehow, it felt like murder. Actually, Len had brought a second cage with him and thus set two traps some distance apart. Within minutes, he caught one cat in each cage: Brindleson and one of her ginger kittens. Len covered the cages with towels because the darkness apparently calms the cats. It only seemed worse to Arnold and Molly, however. Len carried his catches off to his vehicle and drove away. He explained later that the kitten had been sent off immediately to "foster parents" who were very experienced at befriending kittens which could confidently be offered to suitable applicants very soon thereafter. The kitten would be chipped and, in due course, neutered and would have a happy new home. Arnold and Molly basically believed all this but still felt like murderers. As for Brindleson, being older (probably about ten months old by this time), she might take longer to domesticate but such was the aim. Molly later found out that her domestication was taking much longer than the RSPCA people liked and the Forbutts were left with the thought that she might be euthanised eventually even if that was not true. After a couple of weeks or so, Len returned with one cage and successfully caught one more kitten. Once again, it was a ginger one from Brindleson's litter.

When it came to feeding time, Arnold wondered how well Brindle's kittens would take to Brindleson's one remaining baby – the black one. He needn't have worried, they all got on well together and Brindle herself seemed happy to take it under her wing. Do cats have wings, one might ask? Ask Arnold: he has a feel for that kind of thing.

For the sake of security and best practice, please note that the cat count was now six.

'Which are boys and which girls?' asked Molly one day. 'Not sure,' replied Arnold, once bitten, twice shy.

As the days and weeks went by, what had seemed rather like a blur of cats at mealtimes became rather more ordered and recognisable. Molly and Arnold began to give the kittens names, almost without realising that they were doing so, nevertheless avoiding any fixings of gender. The two ginger kittens were distinguished by one having wonderful, large, droopy whiskers – rather like those of an old man: he came to be called Ginger-Pop. The other had incredibly beautiful markings – swirls – within his gingerness. He looked somewhat as if he was still wearing his pyjamas which was reasonable, when you come to think about it, for all these cats seemed to do was sleep: at least while the humans were around. Accordingly, he or she was named Pee-Jay. The white kitten was called Snowflake and the fawn-cum-pale-ginger one, Molly named Blondie. 'After some pop singer', she told Arnold who remained mystified. What to call Brindleson's smaller black baby? Molly decided upon Small Black Personage. Arnold tried to conform at mealtimes but became confused between Small Black Personage, Black Small Personage, Small Dark Personage and similar garblings. In the end, he asserted his authority and declared the kitten's name to be Personage. All very neat, no sexual definition in any of them. Well, hardly. All bets covered. Arnold was a learner.

Getting up at six a.m. so that the cats could be fed promptly, set a back-stiffening role for our hero. He didn't mind waking up that early but would have much preferred to wallow a while. But show some backbone, he did. He cut up some bread for the birds – something he had been doing for years now; and even bought grapes to supplement their meagre diet (for, after all, how would these wild creatures survive in the wild?) – and as ballast for the cats. He filled a small bowl with milk, he added dry cat food on top of the bread in each of two bowls (well, it was increasingly difficult for six cats to gather around only one bowl in mutual peace and harmony) and, finally, topped off each bowl with wet food from a tin.

'Lamb casserole! Smells delicious!' Each morning he would inform his audience of the delights in store as his nostrils involuntarily attempted total closure.

Arnold got his reward, however, not in heaven, for he wasn't ready for that yet, but when he opened that door onto the deck and was greeted by six mewling cats jumping up towards him, simultaneously purring fit to bust. As time went by, Arnold even managed to give one or another cat a wee stroke before it realised what was happening and moved off, but only temporarily. It seemed as if the whole deck out there was a swaying, heaving furball of gratitude and love. Rather like a live rave, thought Arnold, although he had never been to one in person, only via television. Anthropomorphism is a wonderful thing.

Arnold regularly complained about the soaring costs of feeding this lot.

'I work my fingers to the bone...' he would bleat, with little hope of, or interest in, receiving any sympathy, even from Molly.

'Yes, fayther,' she would respond wearily.

It was what pensions were for, after all, and that early morning bathe within the cat ballet had imprinted itself in Arnold's brain. He was hooked.

After feeding the cats and birds, Arnold turned his attention to breakfast for Molly and himself which they were wont to imbibe upstairs in bed while watching so-called news on the telly.

'How many were in this morning?' Molly would enquire, her gaze fixed upon a long-running advertisement for gym equipment requiring but fourteen minutes each day of your time. Fourteen minutes from actors who were so slim and muscular that they clearly had no need of the damn equipment anyway.

'Who hasn't got fourteen minutes?' asked the man on the box.

'Time enough to feed the cats,' Arnold mumbled.

'Full house,' Arnold commonly reported to Molly, though often he would note the absence of Brindle from the pack.

'Is she off whoring again?' Molly would ponder aloud. It was, indeed, something they both feared and expected in equal measure.

'They've got to go,' was often Molly's follow-up. Arnold grunted, for there was little of real substance in these exchanges. And anyway, his boiled egg would be getting cold.

A second sentimental wave greeted Molly and Arnold when they finally made it downstairs for morning coffee. Two or three – on one occasion, four – of the cats had piled into a small wooden cat box Arnold had put there, after been bequeathed it by a good friend some years earlier.

'We'll never use that any more,' Arnold had confidently predicted after the death of the loving cat which they had inherited from Gordon and Mavis some years back. Arnold was indeed perspicacious, as we have seen on many occasions already.

The sight of a knot of mixed fur with multi-coloured tails and legs poking out at alarming angles always brought knots to the stomachs of both Molly and Arnold. The kids were well-fed and happy. That was what this was all about. The Forbutts could drink their morning coffees in peace and contentment. Like the cats, really. You know, that's not anthropomorphism; it's more like being avatars for the furry ones. Arnold and Molly were totally on a string. They had completely surrendered. And they knew it. That is the real difference between these species, you see. The cats always know it will be so, while humans only come to a recognition of their condition after their superior brain power grasps the situation.

Life continued thus for some months, during which the young cats continued to grow, the cat food bills mounted up, and the degree of feline-human bonding strengthened. Arnold slipped in more and more gentle strokes during the early morning feeding frenzy but was aware that his success rested firmly upon the juxtaposition of food and cat-hunger. Furthermore, it only worked really with Ginger-Pop and, possibly, Blondie. Snowflake, for example, was having none of it and Pee-Jay never came within a metre of any human. One morning, as the whole gang of youngsters were waiting for their breakfast – Brindle being away at that time (and what was she doing, one might ask?) – the sneck on the door to the deck slipped from Arnold's fingers and made a sudden loud noise which startled the waiting cats. It was probably Pee-Jay who was most disturbed, for he took off at such speed, communicating his angst to his fellows so well, that the deck took on the appearance of a starburst. Pee-Jay himself (yes, both Arnold and Molly were pretty sure Pee-Jay was male: something to do with Molly catching sight of his balls one day) flew off nearly horizontally for several metres before running under his favourite fig tree. Even so, the others did their very best to follow suit. Arnold opened the door, bearing two heaped bowls of sweet-smelling delights, and called out firmly but gently to the scattered throng.

'Oh, don't be silly. I'm sorry, the sneck slipped. No-one's going to hurt you! Here's your breakfast. Come on now.'

Their fright lasted a further two seconds at least before they returned to devour their grub. The whole incident, however, did illustrate the nervousness of the cats with respect to humans. Certainly to Arnold, although things weren't much better for Molly. It was such a disappointment and the Forbutts were convinced that all of Brindle's offspring had learned this distrust of humans directly from their mother. Arnold observed one day that their fear of him was probably greater than of Molly, despite the fact that he was the one who had most contact with them: for which read, gave most food to them.

'I reckon Brindle was badly treated by some man in the past,' he opined one day. Molly thought that was likely. Even if that were so, however, they saw no way to overcome the cats' fear other than patience and quiet talk.

'I could try reasoning with them, mither,' Arnold suggested one day. 'Aye, feyther,' Molly replied, and the conversation died the death.

In all this time, of course, the Forbutts' affection for the cats was increasing. It wouldn't be an exaggeration to describe their feelings as love. That didn't stop them offering them up to their special friend, Martina, who popped in for drinkipoos every other week.

'Oo, they're lovely,' she would coo as she watched Arnold giving the furballs their tea.

'Which five would you like?' Arnold would ask each time, but Martina wouldn't bite. There were endless conversations between the besotted Forbutts and their many and varied guests along the lines of, 'They've got to go. We are too old to look after them and, in any case, we'd have to catch them first and have them doctored and, anyway, we can't look after so many… Blah, blah, blah…' And the love grew. It seemed that Blondie, at least, was getting a touch more friendly; and maybe Ginger-Pop too. Or were the Forbutts imagining the whole thing?

The RSPCA seemed to have washed their hands of the whole matter.

Despite having expressed considerable concern originally over there being a coven of wild cats in that suburb, they repeatedly failed to return Molly's increasingly frequent calls for help. Eventually, it became obvious that they were doing so on purpose. Len came no more. 'What are we going to do?' wailed Molly. Arnold stared into the abyss.

Well, it happened eventually. It was bound to. Brindle disappeared for a while, seemingly to the delight of her offspring who then got on so well together, constructing a wall of solidarity that would have delighted the most ardent unionist. It was a purring, fur wall. There was no way that Arnold could resist. After nearly three weeks' absence, however, Brindle returned and began trying to push her five offspring out. Arnold was incensed, told Brindle very clearly and loudly that it was not going to happen this time, that her kittens (cats now) were staying and if she didn't like it, she could bugger off herself. Brindle cowered for a moment and began her nastiness again. Arnold shouted at her and made to grab her. He had no chance. She ran off. In the old days, she'd have run off a long way and for a long time, but not now. She retreated down the five steps from the deck to the ground below and waited until Arnold went inside and closed the door. Then she came straight back, as if tethered by elastic, and began harassing her children all over again. Arnold opened the door again and threw a small glass of water at her. This time, she retreated for over an hour. Arnold continued to lose these battles for some days before his superior brain suggested a solution. He changed tactics. He fed the cats in two bowls as usual and watched as Brindle would hog most of the food while most of her offspring cowered, waiting until Brindle finished and wandered off. Arnold would then, very quietly, open the door once more and put down a third bowl of food, waving the kids in to eat. He would watch in exasperation as the situation dawned so slowly in the brains of these beautiful furry beasts until they, very hesitatingly, got into it. Arnold whispered to them, 'Come on. It's yours! Go for it!' He told Molly about his exasperation.

'Can't rush things, feyther,' she replied, 'there's only one brain cell amongst the lot of them and they take it in turns to use it.'

'It probably spends most of its time outside their heads in transit,' Arnold suggested.

Molly and Arnold were only too well aware of what had caused this frisson between Brindle and her offspring. There was clearly a new litter somewhere. They kept looking out of the side window which gave onto that part of the garden in front of Brindle's previous happy nursery behind those bushes. You remember, where she had raised the present four. After a few days of intermittent observation, they caught sight of Brindle playing with a pure white kitten. So there was the evidence. Only one kitten this time. Perhaps that was the way of it? Numbers decrease in later litters? Yes, that must be it. They had temporarily forgotten, it seems, that, within their own experience of Brindle, she had produced first two and then four kittens. So their logic was, perhaps, a little weak. Next day, they got an SMS from Mavis, next door. 'Just seen three white kittens in your garden.' Arnold replied, 'We were aware of one.'

'Well, she's had triplets,' came the reply. There was a distinct coldness in this communication.

Molly and Arnold kept looking out of that side window. In due course, they were rewarded (is that the correct word here?) by the sight of three white kittens plus one grey.

'Just spotted a fourth,' Arnold messaged Mavis.

'Probably explains the soil being dug up in our vegetable patch,' snapped the reply.

Arnold sent, 'Sorry.' He didn't know what else to say. 'We don't know what to do,' he sent.

Arnold sent, 'Sorry.' He didn't know what else to say. 'We don't know what to do,' he added.

'Catch the breeder!' came the reply, as cold as ice.

Arnold didn't dare point out that he had absolutely no idea how he was to do that. Brindle was as wily as they come. He showed the SMS exchange to Molly who became very upset, for she really didn't want to upset the Dunports. They had been friends for over twenty years. But she and Arnold really had no idea how to proceed in all this. Their customary banter ceased, they continued to feed the earlier brood with Brindle, not forgetting all the while that Brindle's earlier lot were less than happy in their mother's gnarly presence. And thus it continued for several days before Molly announced that there were not three, but four white kittens and one grey in the new litter.

'Oh, how nice,' Arnold observed, 'five is such a nice round number, don't you think?'

For the purposes of security and best practice, it should be pointed out that the cat count around the place was now up to eleven.

'This has become ridiculous,' Arnold observed. He was rather good at stating the obvious, was our Arnold.

For the purposes of security and best practice, by the way, it should be pointed out that the cat food bill was now sky-high. More significant, perhaps, is that Arnold was beginning to find it a great strain carrying eight tins from the supermarket along with his regular groceries. Perhaps I hadn't mentioned Arnold's age before? At this juncture in the tale, he was knocking on seventy-eight. Of late, his legs had become very weak and he had begun to walk like a bandy-legged old man he remembered from his childhood. So eight tins and the rest was quite a tall order. He'd bought eight, by the way, because there had been a special offer when buying four, and he had to make full use of that. Arnold had spotted this special offer within a microsecond of reaching the appropriate shelf. Arnold has an eye for these things.

The new kittens seem to have been constructed in a different way from their elder siblings. That lot had been pretty active, you remember, running and jumping all over the garden, to Arnold's and Molly's delight of course, but when only a week or so old, they were cautious and far less agile later in their brief lives so far. This new brood were seemingly made of India rubber. They positively bounced as they hopped from place to place, they were far more daring than the old lot (or more stupid), and they delighted Arnold and Molly all over again. Note that: all over again. Arnold refused to give them names, for that way points the way to hell. Like last time. Meanwhile, the delicate fronds of the spirea simply quivered with delight as the kittens dashed in and out of their new-found hiding place.

Molly told her friends in book club about the cat problem and struck gold. Gold. Liz, who was owner/guardian/feeder to both cats and dogs understood Molly and Arnold's problem completely, especially since Molly's inability to walk far these days due to an arthritic back had been empathised with on several occasions. She also recognised Arnold's ageing problems and she had some inkling of how much the two of them cared for these cats. She volunteered her long-suffering husband, Henry, and herself, to catch the cats and to take them to the RSPCA. They were well aware of how many cats there were. They would begin operations in a week's time, she said, after they had borrowed a couple of cages from friends. Meanwhile, Arnold was able to borrow a third cage from another neighbour, John Woodbine. John had made no secret of his dislike of cats but, on the other hand, neither had he made overt complaints against the Forbutts' brood. Something to do with peace and quiet with the neighbours, I should think. Arnold had mixed feelings about all this cage business. So had Molly. Neither spoke about them. The memories of Brindleson and two of her kittens being caught all that time ago were acute. How had they fared? Were they now in new homes? Did they miss their mother/brother/sister? Did they remember them? Did they hate Arnold and Molly for allowing them to be caught? Did they remember them?

'They'll be fine,' Molly assured Arnold. Or herself.

It had to be done. The day came when Henry and Liz appeared with two, very large dog cages. Arnold helped to bait them, and Henry decided where to place them all.

'Give us a call when you catch any,' Liz said, as they departed to live their own lives for the rest of the day.

Arnold then left home on his regular daily shopping trip. On his return, he drove his car into the garage, switched off the engine, and got out, ready to take his groceries into the house. He wasn't straining to hear or anything. Indeed, he had temporarily forgotten about the cages.

He heard a cat crying. It was a pitiful sound, quite unlike the snarls or miaows with which he was only too familiar. The cat was crying for God's sake, not crying out. A great difference, thought Arnold. He hurried into the kitchen to deposit his groceries. Out of the corner of his eye – but in truth, he had swivelled his eye in that direction involuntarily – he caught a glimpse of the imprisoned cat. It was Ginger-Pop.

Oh God! Arnold inwardly wailed, it had to be you, didn't it?

'We've caught Ginger-Pop,' he shouted to Molly who was busy elsewhere in the house.

'I'll phone Liz,' was all she said, reporting back that Liz said to wait a while, in case they caught another.

There were no other takers by the time that Liz and Henry appeared. They transferred Ginger-Pop to a travelling basket and took him off. He objected strongly the whole time, even though Arnold had covered his cage with a towel in an attempt to calm him. Liz had said that it would. Arnold was unsure whether Ginger-Pop himself understood this, however. Oh, by the way, Ginger-Pop was a male. The folks at the RSPCA confirmed that. Liz reported back to Molly that he had been introduced into a much larger cage (his own room, or some such soothing phrase) where he had curled up on a large blanket and gone to sleep.

These words calmed Arnold and Molly somewhat, although Arnold wondered just how true they were.

'It has to be done, luv,' Molly said to Arnold. He nodded and busied himself with various domestic tasks. Later, he joined Molly and was reading a book when there came an enormous crash from outside the window. He looked outside at where Henry had placed another cage.

Molly phoned Liz. 'We've caught two of the little white kittens,' she reported. A few metres away, Brindle looked on, her other brood in tow, having already discovered that there was absolutely nothing she could do to help her captured offspring. 'What is she thinking?' Arnold wondered, always ready to anthropomorphise and torture himself. Somewhat later that afternoon, Liz came to transfer these two white kittens to her carrying basket. They had other ideas and fought like the little rubber furballs they were. One got away. Liz departed with just one. The cages were brought inside the garage for the night. Neither Molly nor Arnold could stomach the thought of any of the cats being held captive all night, especially as those nights were turning rather cool now as winter approached.

Arnold put out all three cages next morning. No one was caught that morning. Obviously, the cats were getting the point, Arnold reasoned, for he had a nose for these things. Then he checked again, for he had depended on his ears rather than his eyes. Just as well that he did, for he discovered that Pee-Jay had been caught in the cage which Henry had placed behind the fig tree. Pee-Jay was silent and not struggling to escape. Quite different behaviour from Ginger-Pop's. Molly phoned Liz. Liz said she'd leave it a while to see if another cat should be caught. Some good time later, Liz phoned to say that she would take Pee-Jay and any other to a local vet instead of directly to the RSPCA. That vet, apparently, was prepared to take stray and other cats overnight on their way to the RSPCA. Liz's decision meant that Pee-Jay would be held in his cage for another three hours or so. Neither Molly nor Arnold were happy about that but could do nothing about it. Arnold, in particular, fell silent for the rest of the afternoon and early evening. He had put a towel over Pee-Jay's cage in the hope of calming him. Trouble was, he couldn't rid his mind of the image of Pee-Jay huddled in the cage, nor of his obvious distress as Arnold came up to him to envelop the cage. Arnold hoped that being shaded from the light would calm Pee-Jay. It certainly did not calm Arnold. By the time he and Molly had sat down to dinner and were watching the news on the television, the light had gone outside. For Molly and Arnold, the telly was little more than moving pictures, really, for neither could stop thinking about Pee-Jay outside in his cage. Arnold asked Molly to phone Liz again to ask what was happening. Liz heard the anguish in Molly's voice. Indeed, Molly was beginning to lose it. She reported to Arnold that Liz was on her way, and then burst into tears.

'I wasn't going to do this,' she sobbed, 'I have tried so hard not to do this. I really have.' Arnold, too had lost control and his tears flowed like a waterfall.

He couldn't speak. They sat like that, together, trying to calm themselves. After half an hour Arnold could stand it no longer and rushed outside to check on Pee-Jay.

He had been taken away. In his cage, as Liz had promised. She phoned shortly afterwards to say that it had all gone smoothly, that the vet had put Pee-Jay into a warm room and that he had been fed and was now curled up in a basket. Arnold and Molly calmed down a little and were able to distract themselves with a little rubbishy television for the rest of the evening. Liz and Henry were going away for the next couple of days so there would be a respite from all this slaughter for a while, for that was how Arnold saw their actions.

How would the remaining cats react to missing some of their number? How could one tell? They seemed a little quieter than normal, perhaps, but Arnold found it difficult to be sure. They came in for their meals, they slept together, they argued together, they purred at mealtimes. Wednesday, Thursday and Friday were cage-free days, and everyone calmed down a bit. Saturday turned out to be wet until early afternoon, so the cages weren't put out then either. That meant, Arnold and Molly assumed, that attempts to catch more cats would be left until Monday because the RSPCA centre was closed on Sundays. Arnold was quietly pleased about that for, although he was totally aware that the job had to be done, it meant that his gang of reprobates could enjoy just a few days more chez Forbutt. Or, to put it another way, Arnold could enjoy their company for a bit longer.

Wrong again, I'm afraid! Liz phoned Molly to explain that she and Henry would come to set the traps again on Sunday because they could take cats to that same local vet, ready for passing onto the RSPCA when they opened. So the whole business began again. As Arnold was helping Liz to place the third trap – in the side garden, this time – Liz told him that she had just seen the brindle-coloured one. 'In which case,' said Arnold, 'Brindle has seen us and so will be forearmed and will keep well away.' Of course, Brindle was the cat they were keenest to catch, really, for she was the "breeder" and the least domesticated. Mind you, the chances of ultimate domesticity in someone else's hands were also the poorest, with an obvious conclusion. Anyway, she'd seen the trap being set, so... Arnold had a nose for these things.

About one hour later, Molly reported hearing the trap nearest the house going off. Arnold checked. Brindle had been caught, together with one of her white kittens! The kitten wasn't heavy enough to activate the trap and Brindle had obviously gone in to rescue her baby, tripped the trap and so been caught in a wonderful act of motherhood. Well, that was how the Forbutts interpreted the whole thing. Arnold covered the cage with a towel while Molly phoned Liz. Both Molly and Arnold found it emotionally easier to deal with this capture because they had not yet named the kittens – which meant they had not yet formed any strong bond with them – and Brindle's repeated nastiness towards her previous brood, however natural it undoubtedly was, had soured the Forbutts' view of their original protégé. Obviously, the love had not run too deep there. Liz and Henry came to pick up Brindle and her kitten quickly this time, Liz having learned just how wrapped up in all these cats Molly and Arnold were. They rang soon afterwards to say that the vet's facilities were full, and that the RSPCA would not open again until Tuesday because of a public holiday. Arnold and Molly had discovered since their emigration to this country of their retirement, that Australia has more public holidays than you could point a stick at, as the locals are wont to say. Anyway, Liz and Henry, true friends that they were, stated that they would care for Brindle and her kitten until then. Obviously, they would have preferred not to have to do that, but they did it, nevertheless.

The cat count was now down to six, three from Brindle's previous and Brindleson's first litters, and three from Brindle's latest litter: in short, three cats and three kittens. The traps were put aside for a few days. Of course, there was now the question of whether the little kittens had acquired enough experience to come up to the deck and tuck into whatever Arnold put in a bowl for them, bearing in mind that their mother wasn't there to shoo off the larger cats so as to give them a chance. Arnold was determined to put on a show for all the cats in his charge, to appear as if nothing had happened and to encourage the littlies to partake at mealtimes. He reckoned that the next few days were likely to be difficult. Especially so, in view of a patch of unusually cold and wet weather which descended upon the whole of the south-eastern part of the country at that time.

Well, bless them, the three older cats came to eat together in relative harmony and the little kittens showed some pluck as they ascended the steps to the deck and attempted to insert their little heads into the food bowls. The grey kitten proved to be the best at this, the cats moving aside a little to allow him in. The white kittens were more wary, standing close to the circle of their elder siblings, waiting for a break. Brindle wasn't there to push for them, and they were unsure how to proceed. Arnold tried waving to them through the window in encouragement but, at first, they took this as a threat and ran away.

'This is going to take some time,' Arnold reported.

Actually, it took less time than he expected. Hunger won out and, by the next mealtime, all three kittens had got the hang of it. They had to defer to the cats, but they did get a meal. Afterwards, Arnold noticed Blondie playing with one of the kittens, jumping up and down while the littlie ran in circles around her. Arnold had decided that Blondie was female, by the way: as we well know, Arnold has an eye for these things. It warmed his heart to see such mothering. He reckoned that he would put her name up for a medal or something.

Trapping began again after a few days and was almost immediately successful with the capture of the grey and one of the white kittens which Henry took away almost immediately. The cat count, therefore, was now down to four. 'Oh, that it could all be over soon,' thought Arnold, dreading the next days.

The weather, however, brought a hiatus to proceedings. Unseasonable cold and rain persuaded the cats to stay under the house where they kept warm from Arnold's inefficient heating ducts.

'Am I supposed to be heating all Australia?' he would moan without actually doing anything to fix the problem. He knew there was thermal leakage (he thought that was a rather upmarket phrase for a tear in the ducting) but, with lightning-fast logic, rationalised it all with, 'Well, at least the cats can get warm.' Arnold: if you hadn't deliberately attracted Brindle in the first place, you wouldn't have any cats to keep warm. He acknowledged this but then immediately thought of the cat's ballet first thing each morning.

After a week, there came a break in the rain and Liz and Henry suggested resuming the quest. Henry would arrive at six-thirty a.m. to put out and set the traps and to place dark towels over them so as to make the cages seem like interesting caves. Someone at the RSPCA centre had suggested that move. Arnold slept little that night, realising that he was to prepare breakfast in the morning while somehow ignoring Snowflake and Personage calling to him through the kitchen window. Not just calling but actually being there on the window ledge.

'Come on, Dad,' he imagined them thinking, 'Make with the breakfast. It's cold out here and we're hungry.'

He knew he should stop inventing conversations with the cats, but they suggested themselves all the time. Truth was, he enjoyed these little fictions. Tomorrow, however, he was going to leave the cats without any breakfast. He was to put food into the traps, the plan being to entice the cats into them using both hunger and curiosity – the dark caves and all that – as bait. All night, Arnold thought about all this and dreaded facing those cats next morning.

When morning did come and he finally dragged himself down to the kitchen, he was let off the hook for some time. Clearly, the cats fancied a sleep-in themselves, so Arnold got on with taking saucers of food and towels into the garage where Henry was to collect them as he set the traps. Arnold then busied himself with his usual breakfast duties for him and Molly. He was only a little way along with those tasks when Snowflake appeared on the window ledge. Arnold tried to ignore him/her for a while but felt awful. Like the coward he was, he ran from the kitchen and escaped into the toilet downstairs, hoping that, by the time he re-emerged, Henry would have arrived and scared away Snowflake and any other cats which had emerged by then. It worked. As Arnold climbed the stairs back into the kitchen, he spotted Henry busily working outside. There was no sign of the cats. Like the proverbial thief in the night, Arnold finished making breakfast. Well, that was the plan but the whole process took too long. Henry had gone and after a while, Snowflake reappeared. Not on the window ledge, thank God, but on the deck. Arnold pretended not to notice the cat while he hurried along. As he finally completed his tasks and was about to carry the breakfast tray upstairs, Snowflake appeared on the window ledge and looked plaintively at him.

Arnold took to the hills. Literally. He carried the tray upstairs and out of sight. He wondered how to describe what he was feeling at that moment. It soon became only too clear to him. He had betrayed the cats.

'Henry's been,' he told Molly as he put down the breakfast tray. She wisely said nothing. They watched the morning breakfast show as they consumed their own breakfast, a breakfast which those four adorable cats had not been offered.

When Arnold finally went down into the kitchen to make coffee a couple of hours later, he carefully peeked to see if any of the traps had been sprung. None had.

You're not catching us that easily, he could hear the cats calling in his over-active imagination, tormenting him.

Oh, God, how long will this go on for? he thought. If only I hadn't encouraged Brindle in the first place... What a silly and pointless thought, Arnold. You have nurtured all these lovely cats for months and given them a wonderful start in their lives. You didn't quite win their trust, but you were well on the way. It will surely be so much easier for "professional" carers to domesticate them after all this. Won't it?

Betrayed was still the word.

By mid-afternoon, he could stand it no longer, announcing to Molly that he would feed the cats properly. Now. Although Molly had directed him to give them very short rations so that they would seek out the food in the traps, she acceded to Arnold's announcement. The cats had won. Both Molly and Arnold had had enough. They didn't know what was to be done next except that those cold, hungry cats simply had to be shown some love. The cats purred, ate, yawned and groomed themselves. Their humans had been put in their place.

Well, all well and good, but that didn't solve the problem so now Arnold and Molly returned to their accustomed state of depression. But that depression was far more acceptable than the despair and guilt they had been feeling before. Arnold began imagining scooping up one or more of the cats while they were eating, passing them to Liz or Henry inside who could them put them into their carrying basket. Molly thought little of the plan, Arnold could think of nothing else. Indeed, he spent the whole night thinking about it.

2

Word got around that the Forbutts were nurturing feral cats. Not a few, but dozens of them and when I say "around", I mean that seemingly everyone in the street knew about it. Typically, for social media in particular and gossip in general, the information being pedalled was deficient in two important respects: it was grossly exaggerated, and it was completely out of date. But once the seed is sown, it takes root immediately and we all know how difficult some weeds are to eradicate. Meanwhile, the weed spreads. At first, neither Arnold nor Molly heard anything about the rumour, the story, the defamation. Arnold did notice that neighbours who used to wave to him from their gardens as he drove past for his daily grocery shopping, no longer did so. Somewhat later, he caught sight of the children of a couple way down the street pointing at him and jeering. Arnold pulled up a hundred metres or so further along the road, got out, and walked around his car to see if there was some mud on it, or something else amiss. He found nothing, however, and drove off in some puzzlement. Then a crude note appeared in the Forbutts' letter box.

'We don't need feral cats round here,' it said, and added, 'they should be exterminated.' It wasn't signed.

Arnold already felt, of course, that he had exterminated their cats, even though he knew that not to be so, so that vicious message hit home. He learned later that even nastier messages were being posted on Twatter, but Arnold had never signed up to Twatter, Face-off or any other of those media serving as loudhailers for those who imagine their voices will not be heard in the conventional ways which used to be called discourse – that is, speaking to one another – and who imagine that it is their God-given right to outshout all others. He thus never heard or read about the disgraceful garbage sent his way; this was undoubtedly a good thing. However, many others did. Not only those living elsewhere along the street, but goodness knows how many other people in his suburb, or his city, or his country, or the world. Such are the evils of those wonderful antisocial media. It was the case, however, that some extraordinarily vicious things were being written about him. Anonymously, of course.

However, without his knowledge and equally behind his back, Arnold's reputation was simultaneously being defended, for one near-neighbour, Andrew Manning, let fly at those hurtful gossips. He and his wife, Nina, had befriended the Forbutts some years earlier and knew the true story of those cats. Furthermore, Andrew was a most fair-minded man and was not going to sit idly by while his friend was being insulted and maligned. Andrew made his views known on Twatter very clearly. He informed the menacing cowards of the truth of the matter in very great detail, for he and Nina knew all about it, including the fact that even before the first person to attack Arnold Forbutt had disseminated his bile, every last one of the cats Arnold and Molly had so lovingly cared for had been sent off to the RSPCA to be domesticated and re-homed. And the fact that, included amongst their number, was the original abandoned cat who had bred all the rest. In short, a pre-existing problem of abandoned cats in that suburb had been solved by the very people now being vilified by an ignorant, stupid, screeching mob. Andrew pulled no punches. He was disgusted by what he saw as outright character assassination.

By the time that Arnold got to hear about the popular attack upon him in the social media, he simultaneously heard of Andrew's defence. He and Molly immediately invited the Mannings round for lunch, by way of thanks but also to learn all about what had been going on behind their backs and they were as astounded as they were grateful. Lunches with the Mannings, by the way, were regular, although those provided by Nina and Andrew were always populous affairs. They appeared to the Forbutts as people with more friends than you could point a stick at. Arnold liked that phrase, by the way, and remembered when and where he had first heard it: from an Aussie friend in England, years before the Forbutts had emigrated to Australia. Arnold had a tendency to remember little details like that. He had an ear for them. He also thought it was an essentially Australian phrase until he discovered that it was in popular use in England in the late days of the nineteenth century, if not earlier. Arnold was always learning things like that. Anyway, the Forbutts and the Mannings got on famously together. Arnold always referred to Andrew's Fijian-born wife as a Fijian princess, for she was very beautiful. She seemed not to mind. In any case, it appeared that all of the Manning's other friends agreed with this sentiment. Luncheon parties chez Manning were very loving affairs. Unbeknown to the Forbutts, Andrew and Nina continued their defence of the Forbutts in conversations with their many friends and, in time, the Forbutt name began to shine. Nor did it just come to be repaired, mind you, but to become burnished. The fools who had earlier posted obscenities about Arnold on the web were now lauding him as a defender of the suburb against demon feral cats. One detail in the ether stayed the same, however. There were, apparently, hundreds of these feral beasts: so many that they had threatened to overwhelm all other creatures in the area. It seemed that the liars had to have something to cling to, something on which to hang their venom or their adulation, depending upon the direction in which the wind of public prejudice was blowing at any given time. But now, Arnold had become the conqueror and hero.

Arnold remained adamant that he would not sign up to Twatter or the rest of those facilities, but his curiosity about what was being said about him grew. He refused to ask anyone, however, for to do so, in his view, would be akin to his signing up to social media. Arnold was nothing if not consistent. He had an eye for consistency. He had to take notice, however, when he and Molly received an invitation to a street party which was being convened in their honour. Surely, thought Arnold, this is going a bit far. It was clear, however, that they could not refuse to attend. If so many people were going to the trouble and expense of setting up a street party in their honour, it would be churlish in the extreme to decline the invitation. And thus, it came to pass. It was being held in the (very large) garage of the home of Deno and Angela Garcetti. There were dozens of people there – truly, this time – all with a glass in their hand, enjoying the gathering. As Molly and Arnold arrived and were spotted by those already gathered, glasses were raised, and a cataract of cheers rang out. They were as embarrassed as they were touched and tried their best to mix in with everyone in as invisible a way as they could manage. They were not to get away with it, however, for later in the evening, after everyone had enjoyed some food and general chat, Andrew rose to make an address.

'This will be short and to the point,' he began, 'Our friends here, Arnold and Molly Forbutt, have been viciously defamed on social media and yet now, I am very pleased to say, have had their reputations corrected so that they presently stand in the highest esteem: as should be the case. Over a period of roughly two years, Molly and Arnold have befriended a local, abandoned cat and three litters she produced, regularly feeding and loving them all the while. Of late, with the inestimable help of their friends, Liz and Henry Heuvelhijsen, they have managed to transfer all of these cats and kittens to the RSPCA where they have been chipped, de-sexed and found new homes with a variety of loving people. Our area has long been known to the RSPCA as a problem one so far as feral cats are concerned and the Forbutts have solved that problem. Excuse the pun, if I say that, but for the Forbutts, we might have been overrun by people of the feline persuasion. So raise your glasses, ladies and gentlemen, to this patient and caring couple of cat-lovers.'

There were shouts of 'Up the Forbutts', and 'Molly and Arnold', and all that sort of thing. Arnold heard them all. He has an ear for that sort of thing. Molly gave Andrew a hug for his speech and happiness flowed all over the place. Then everyone got back to some serious drinking.

It was during that relaxed time that a stranger sidled up to Arnold.

'Mr. Forbutt,' he said, 'my name is Clive Nassen. I represent our local newspaper. I wonder if you would be willing to give us an interview and to be heard on our associated local radio station.'

Thinking that he might be able to use the occasion to lambast social media, Arnold agreed to Clive's request. Silly man.

It was agreed to report on the Forbutts' trials and tribulations in writing in the first instance. The report of that interview soon appeared in the DayNews and served as the basis for a subsequent live interview on air. Arnold was given every opportunity to sound off about the evils of social media – and he did – before Clive pointed out that

Arnold himself was exploiting the power of a broadcasting medium to disseminate his personal views about another medium which was beloved by millions of other people. What right had he to get so uppity?

Arnold saw immediately that he was in the soup. Or something like that. He had a nose for these things. Yet again, his nose seemed to work just a tad behind events. It was a pity, really, that Arnold had never really understood social media, but then he was an old man, a fact which he hoped might excuse many sins. Arnold pointed out, however and quite rightly, that he wasn't hiding behind anonymity like the cowards on Twatter, for example. Arnold had absolutely no idea just what a fizzer he had lit. It didn't take long before evidence of a reading and listening audience was made manifest. That evidence came in the form of readers' letters in response to Clive Nassen's written article and as twots and such on the social media. The readers' letters were all signed, of course, for newspapers do not publish anonymous material. More than half of those letters expressed a degree of agreement with Arnold's sentiments; occasionally, markedly so. The other group, however, pointed out that they were happy to sign their names but thought that Arnold's views were snobbish, hoity-toity and, using a local Australian epithet, that Arnold was up 'imself. There were many more twots on Twatter. Some were signed properly, some not. Some were written in what might just be called English (no disrespect to non-English speakers intended here) while rather more resembled the outpourings of raving lunatics with dysentery. Almost all of these expressed the view that Arnold was mad, weird or unfit for human consumption. It took only one day more before some joker posted a short piece on Tak-Tik in which he jeered at Arnold in rap. Arnold, of course, had no knowledge of any of these things except for those letters in the DayNews. The rest of the world and his wife did, though. The rap ditty on Tak-Tik became viral within three days. Arnold learned that it garnered several million "likes". He knew what a "like" was, did Arnold. Just because he refused to twot and whatnot, did not mean that he was completely gaga. Arnold learned that jeering messages were being posted from all points of the globe. Even Arnold's arrogance about social media failed to protect his psyche from so intense a battering. Molly was appalled.

Arnold did not scurry away into a corner. Pity. Instead, he wrote to the new owner of Twatter, a most successful entrepreneur by the name of Noel Dusk. He knew, by the way, that Noel Dusk was one of a family of triplets, named Noel, Leon and… Arnold couldn't remember the third's name and nothing memorable seemed possible just by rearranging those four letters. He also recalled that an early business success of Noel Dusk was the creation of that company, PayUpPal, with which he remembered having a run-in with, some while back. With people pretending to be representing PayUpPal, if you remember. Mr. Dusk had created the company from nothing and sold it, after only a very few years, for hundreds of millions of dollars. Since then, Mr. Dusk had moved into space. Well not actually moved there in any physical way (but watch this space, by the way) and that he had constructed a company which sent rockets into space on a commercial footing. Initially, it had seemed ridiculous to Arnold that private enterprise could take on the likes of NASA, for Arnold had a nose for that sort of thing and he was in no way shy of telling people so. But things turned out differently, and Noel Dusk was now head of a company which had successfully designed, manufactured, launched (and relaunched) larger and ever larger rockets into orbit around the Earth. He had sent astronauts to the International Space Station (and successfully returned them whole and well to Earth), launched many hundreds of small satellites whose purpose was to create a worldwide net of relay stations for disseminating electronic messages. 'Like the twots on Twatter,' Arnold explained to Molly. Mr. Dusk had completed this latter enterprise by actually purchasing Twatter. So his control over all that sort of thing seemed pretty well complete to our friend. Mr. Dusk, meanwhile, had filled in his spare time building electric cars which worked by carrying their fuel with them in enormously heavy batteries so that much of it was spent hauling themselves around. The point being made here, Arnold was only too happy to explain to the interested passer-by, was that engines burning petrol – or gas, as Americans confusingly call it – only carry the combustible element around, taking the necessary oxygen to burn it, as required, directly from the free air around at the time. Arnold thought a far better idea would be to make use of hydrogen, carried in much lighter fuel-cells and, as with petrol engines, burn it as required with air from the great outdoors, only this time to produce harmless water vapour. And, like Mr. Dusk's batteries, the fuel is hopefully replenished from solar sources. Arnold had a view about these things. Whatever Arnold's learned views on these matters might be, however, the ever-resourceful Noel Dusk had, by now, built an empire around his batteries, his electric vehicles, his information networks and his space rockets. And probably, Arnold mused, many other enterprises which he had forgotten about. Mr. Dusk was, by now, the richest person in the world and was a man with many other ambitions left over to astound us all. When he found time to sleep, was anyone's guess. Apart, perhaps, from the famous tyrants of history, Arnold mused, Noel Dusk has probably achieved more than any other person in history; if not quite yet then certainly very soon. And that's why Arnold had chosen to write to Noel Dusk. 'Go straight to the top,' was Arnold's motto. 'After all,' he rationalised, 'that's how Dusk himself had advanced. So why not me?' Arnold certainly had an eye for the main chance.

Mr. Dusk might have admired his cheek a little more had Arnold chosen a different path than he did. But Arnold was ever one for straight-shooting. He chose to lambast social media and all who sailed in her; Twatter, in particular.

'Why should people be able to post unsigned twots on any subject they like, especially when those twots were written as poisonous barbs? Mr. Dusk should disembowel the medium immediately,' wrote Arnold. The fact that Noel Dusk had recently spent tens of billions of dollars ('That's billions with a B,' Arnold was wont to point out to all and sundry) to purchase this social medium did serve to make the great man likely unresponsive to Arnold's pleas. 'You should send the whole bloody enterprise into space in one of your mighty rockets,' Arnold concluded. The subtlety of his pitch lent richness to its appeal. Arnold had a way with these things. Arnold was not shy to tell all his friends about how he had lambasted the great Noel Dusk.

To everyone's surprise, Mr. Dusk replied. He pointed out that he had great ambitions with regard to sending things into space and suggested that Arnold might like to visit him in Texas, where his SpaceCentre was situated, and give his advice and observations on that subject. Dusk would pay his fare to Texas. This latter offer was a piece of sheer magic to Arnold's ears and he accepted with alacrity. And so it came to pass that Arnold and Molly (for the invitation had generously included her too) found themselves in the presence of The Great Man but not before they found themselves ensconced in a luxurious motel situated on the perimeter of Dusk's huge SpaceCentre.

Arnold reflected on how many words were spelt these days. Like SpaceCentre, for example, instead of space centre. He knew the reason lay in the bowels of computer program coding where a space (no pun intended) signified the end of something. Names in many coding languages since the early days of four-letter restrictions could now be of more-or-less any length and in any mix of upper and lower case, but they must not contain an embedded space. Instead then, of writing spacecentre as one word with all letters in lower (or upper) case, it was felt that the human parsing process might be assisted by demarking component words with capital letters; hence SpaceStation. Arnold told any passers-by – PassersBy? – all about these tremendously interesting facts whenever he felt that he had a captive audience. His explanations always elided, or more likely failed to recognise, the fact that ordinary English is full of these compound words; like "instead" rather than "in stead": unless, that is, you prefer instead instead of in stead. Arnold didn't always have an eye for these things. It was while he was sounding off to a flunky in the motel about its name, MotelDusk, that a message came through that the great man (GreatMan) would be available for discussions first thing on the morrow. First thing (FirstThing, or FustThing in Arnold's dialect), apparently, was six a.m.. Molly was less than amused.

Dusk turned up in some sort of running gear, towel round his neck and his hair sweaty and tousled. The mere sight of all this enthusiasm turned Arnold's delicate stomach at so early an hour. Noel, as he insisted being called by his guests, shook Molly and Arnold's hands vigorously.

'So glad you agreed to come all this way. I understand, Mr. Forbutt, that you don't like social media. There are many like you, but you won't last long, will you?'

Arnold was so taken aback by such a direct thrust that he was struck dumb.

Dusk continued without, apparently, noticing Arnold's reaction. As far as he was concerned, it was obvious that Arnold was an old man and Dusk was not the sort of person to waste time pretending otherwise.

'I have a proposition to make to you, Arnold – and to you Molly, if you wish to be included – but first, let me show you our magnificent rockets and all the facilities of our SpaceCentre. We're going to cover a lot of ground, so we'll travel in one of my electric buggies. As you can see, it's rather like an oversized golf cart. Do you play golf, Arnold?'

He didn't wait for a reply but continued with his manifestly oft-repeated spiel. They began by watching large sheets of stainless steel being rolled and formed into large, flimsy cylinders.

'These may seem flimsy to you,' Dusk remarked, pointing out the obvious as far as Arnold was concerned, 'but wait till we get to the next part of the shed. 'Shed' was hardly the right word. The cavernous factory seemed to go on for ever. Arnold had never seen so large a building before. 'Here, you will see how those flimsy cylinders are braced internally. They are all to be sections of our great rockets, of course.'

'Of course,' was all Arnold was able to say. He did observe, however, that you could put a double-decker London bus in each of those cylindrical sections; lengthways or sideways. In due course, their party moved beyond the shed into an enormous assembly area outside. There were several huge cranes moving around the place, hauling the shiny, stainless steel cylinders on top of each other as gangs of workmen attached one to another by continuous welds.

'We test the welds several times during construction, of course,' Noel remarked. Each piece of this huge jigsaw was being assembled meticulously, and the final stage of each stood more than fifty stories high, Arnold reckoned. Each rocket body rested on rails and advanced intermittently in such a way that this factory was essentially constructing rockets as Henry Ford had once constructed motor cars (MotorCars). 'At the pointy end of each rocket, there will be a unit eventually capable of carrying three hundred people,' Dusk continued, 'That's the aim for a couple of years hence, of course.'

'Of course,' replied Arnold, his mouth hanging open in a most unbecoming manner.

The tour continued. It was close to nine a.m. when Dusk led the Forbutts into an on-site canteen for breakfast. They passed along a counter, carrying large trays.

'Take whatever you want,' Noel urged his guests, for his part taking plates of grits, waffles with maple syrup, a large thick slice of ham with three fried eggs (sunny side up), a quarter of a pineapple and a large pot of coffee. Molly took a bowl of cornflakes, a small pot of lemon yoghurt and a cup of tea. Arnold set about a bowl of cornflakes, scrambled egg on toast, and a cup of tea. They took their trays to a table and sat amongst many workers of all ranks and specialisms. Noel seemingly knew them all by their first names. Many broke away from their conversations to wish the boss "Morning, Noel" or to ask about some detail of the factory or of the design, but most just gave a perfunctory wave while eagerly pursuing some technical conversation or other whilst scribbling away on scraps of paper. Arnold thought back to the factory and assembly areas they had just seen and wondered where all the money came from to pay for this lot.

'You're wondering where all the money comes from to pay for this lot,' Noel Dusk remarked. 'Well, I'll tell you. At first, it was profits from our battery business but, as we gradually began to succeed in rocketry, the money came increasingly from our charging NASA and other parties for launches. And it's only because we are able to re-use our rockets that we can easily outbid any other corporation on price – and reliability.' He was obviously, and justifiably, very proud of his achievements. 'I am totally confident that we shall be able to send rockets to Mars in two years' time.' Arnold completely believed him. Molly sipped her tea.

Arnold ventured to raise the subject of social media and Twatter.

'Yes, yes. All in good time. I want to show you our plans for colonising Mars first,' Dusk replied. Arnold looked at Molly and shrugged almost imperceptibly. Molly looked at Arnold and barely inclined her head. They ate their breakfasts, watching in wonder as Dusk devoured all of his with obvious relish. Somehow, in between mouthfuls, he asked questions of various members of his design and construction crews while hastily-drawn diagrams were passed back and forth between them. There were many nods and shakes, and excited exchanges. It was obvious that Dusk had a devoted and knowledgeable team. It was equally obvious to Arnold that the thing that marked Dusk out as the great man he was, was that he followed where the science indicated and that he took decisions sharply and decisively. He wouldn't countenance failure and leaped into the future with delight. He might just acknowledge temporary setbacks. Failure, however, was a totally foreign concept to this freakish dynamo of a man. Arnold took some pleasure, however, in finishing his modest breakfast more or less at the same time as Dusk finished his. Arnold noticed such things. It seemed that Noel Dusk noticed these things also for he immediately stood up and urged Arnold and Molly to follow him.

'Let me show you our plans for Mars,' he said. Just like a schoolboy. A multibillionaire schoolboy, that is. He proceeded to outline a five-year plan whose purpose was for mankind to colonise Mars. Arnold had read somewhere about Dusk's ambitions in this regard but had not really taken them seriously and the idea that it might be accomplished in as little as five years seemed absolutely preposterous to our hero. He couldn't help himself and protested that Dusk couldn't expect to achieve his aims so quickly.

'Why not?' asked Dusk and, without waiting for an answer, continued, 'all my life, people have been telling me that my plans were grandiose and could never be successful within one man's lifetime. Well, all my life, I have proved them wrong. All you need is a bit of courage. I have lots of courage. I also have the advantage of being right.'

And modest, Arnold thought, but said nothing.

Dusk's plan was to transport nearly one thousand (one thousand!) people to Mars in the first instance. He reckoned that about that many people would be required to set up a successful colony. He explained how these people would be able to grow food there, to build appropriate accommodation, to collect energy and, in due course, to make fuel for a return flight to Earth. Such a flight might take fifty years to set up, he suggested, but that would have the advantage of focussing his Martians' minds on establishing man's first outpost off Earth – on a different planet – and of ensuring its success.

Arnold was both flabbergasted and disbelieving. 'It will take a special person to lead such an expedition,' he said, 'someone with a relentless focus and determination.' Arnold could not imagine that there was anybody around with such talent who would be prepared to risk all and, even should the expedition survive the journey to the Red Planet and the landing upon it, even if it were successful in establishing its "base camp", Arnold recognised the most obvious flaw in Dusk's plans. 'But who on earth would be happy to leave this planet for good? To be prepared to live, work and to die on Mars?' he exclaimed. Arnold knew he had Noel Dusk on the ropes with that perceptive observation. 'Hey, Mother!' he said quietly to Molly who was standing beside him with her mouth wide open.

'Oh, I've thought about that. You are quite right, Arnold. We shall require a very special person to lead such an enterprise and there is absolutely no point even beginning this task without having found that person up front. Someone very special, someone with determination, someone with an unbroken record of sparkling successes in the face of doubting Thomases. Someone with extraordinary charisma.'

'Well, have you found him?' Arnold asked.

'Me,' replied Dusk, vigorously poking his finger into his own chest. 'Yes, I must put my money, and my life for that matter, where my mouth is. I know of no other human being (HumanBeing) alive today who would be better placed to perform this task.'

Arnold was dumbfounded. He nearly said, 'You really intend to do this?' but saw immediately from Dusk's expression that he meant every word, that Dusk intended for history to remember him as the man who led humans to be the first colonisers of space. Dusk would create PlanetB. His name would live for ever more.

Arnold contemplated the GreatAchiever. 'But what about all his other enterprises? Who would run his battery business, his electric cars, his communications necklace which he had nearly completed setting up in the stratosphere around the Earth?'

'I will, of course! I don't need to be present physically to do all that. I shall be able to communicate with my teams back here on Earth. In any case, I shall need those enterprises to keep going for they will fund our Martian outpost. There will be regular rocket launches from this SpaceStation to keep us supplied with materials, tools and, in the earlier years at least, with food. No, I've thought about all that. I will run the whole thing from Mars myself.'

Arnold remained silent for quite some time. That is, until he remembered how he and Molly had come to be at Dusk's SpaceStation in Texas, USA.

'Why did you invite my wife and I to visit you here, Mr. Dusk?'

3

After all, thought Arnold, all we did was to befriend a stray cat. Just look where that has brought us. Quite right, Arnold: just look.

Noel was about to open his mouth but then thought better of it for a moment. Instead, he beckoned Molly and Arnold over to some pictures and charts on a side wall.

'Look at this display,' he urged them, 'It fills out much of what has been planned so far. I have one or two things to see to right now so, if you'll please excuse me, I would like to leave you with these exhibits for a while so that you can become more clued up about our great enterprise (GreatEnterprise).' Before either Forbutt could ask any more questions, let alone protest, the great man had disappeared from the scene.

'He's still not answered your question, Feyther,' Molly observed.

'No, Mother, nor 'as 'e,' Arnold replied slowly and quietly. It was always a sign that Arnold was thinking deeply when he spoke slowly and quietly like that. Arnold could be quite deep on occasion. As we well know, by this time he had an eye for these matters.

They began to peruse the items on display. It soon became very clear that these were in no way tentative plans for the Martian expedition. They were clearly the result of long, careful deliberation by a large team of people. There were incredibly detailed technical drawings of various forms of accommodation – eating, sleeping, and working areas. There was even a recreation area where both useful and frivolous entertainment would be available. There were scale-drawings of apparatus to collect water, to dispose of waste, mostly to include reprocessing and re-use; there were detailed plans for communications on the Red Planet as well as with mother-Earth (MotherEarth). There were plans for constructing a small SpaceStation near the central area on which Dusk's rockets would land and from which, in due course, presumably depart. It was envisaged that some kilometre or more from the living quarters an industrial centre was to be constructed where fuel was to be synthesised from various raw materials known to be on, or near, the Martian surface. The detail of all this had been worked out to the last nut and bolt.

Arnold and Molly moved further along the display and came to a section devoted to the journey out. It was to take about six months, and ways and means had been devised to help fill that time with both productive, and simply entertaining, things for the captive travellers. After a while, the penny dropped for the Forbutts that, visionary though Noel Dusk might be, he did not expect his companions to share his maniacal temperament. He obviously hoped they shared his vision, but he recognised that they were otherwise quite "normal" people.

'You know, Mother,' Arnold said, 'it occurs to me that our friend Noel is no madman. He doesn't expect members of his teams to be as closely focussed as him and that's just as well because such an enterprise could only have one boss, I reckon. He really is quite realistic in concluding that only he could lead this adventure.'

Molly was a naturally quiet person, as we know, and had been quietly working it all out for herself. 'I think the most amazing thing about Mr. Dusk is the way he marries the visionary with the human. I rather admire the man.'

Well. Molly had said it, so it must be so.

The great man returned after a while. 'What do you think of our exhibits?' he asked but, without giving them any chance to reply, he began to summarise his great project (GreatProject). 'I get so many doubters through here, people who say it's all too dangerous; I'll never get that many volunteers for so dangerous a trip; that the rockets will likely explode or fire off in the wrong direction and be lost for ever; that the world – meaning those on Earth – will lose interest in my colony and send no further support, tools, food or whatever. They dream up one excuse after another for not even beginning the project. They are cowards, weaklings; they're unimaginative. They are little people.'

'Well,' replied Arnold, 'they do have a point, surely. Your dream is truly magnificent, but you cannot deny that it is dangerous. I mean, there are so many things to go wrong. You must admit that. You have to think of pretty much everything beforehand. You get no second chances.'

Dusk was completely unfazed by Arnold's objections and opened his mouth to respond as Arnold hastily continued.

'For instance,' he said, warming to his theme, 'it seems that you now have reliable rockets – and let me say, immediately, how much I admire your achievement – but how many of them exploded on the ground before you got it right? Forgive my saying this, Mr. Dusk, but you are not God. Anyone can make mistakes. Even you.' And, after a pause, continued, 'Even me.'

'Yes, that's fair, Arnold – please do call me Noel – and I don't pretend infallibility, but practice makes perfect. We learned from all those explosions, you know. We didn't make any new attempts without fully understanding their causes and without making appropriate modifications. The point is that we now know how to do it all safely and repeatedly. We have proved that, surely. There are those who make a mistake and promptly repeat that mistake without working it all out. That's not our way, Arnold. Look, I've heard these sorts of criticisms for years with all my projects, but I have always studied my failures and never repeated them. I don't do it all on my own either. I have large teams of very talented scientists and engineers who all make enormous contributions of their own. They, like me, are then subject to the most careful scrutiny by their colleagues and me. And, of course, we repeatedly use extensive testing. Our strength lies in the fact that the financing for it all lies in the hands of one man who has a dream and the courage and determination to see it all through. That's my special talent. And I am only too aware that there are few people in the world like me, that they come along only rarely. That being the case, it is essential that we move with all possible speed. This project must become successful before I die, or it may die. You understand?'

It was Molly who replied. Very quietly. 'Yes, Noel. If you were a despot with power over unimaginable munitions, I would hope to see you assassinated. I don't believe you are such a man. You're probably very selfish. I would guess that you need to be. But I believe you mean what you say, and I also have faith that your judgment is good. You are a great man and I believe that your enterprise will succeed.'

Arnold looked at his wife in some amazement for he had never heard her speak with such calm and authority before.

'Hey, Mother,' he murmured, 'well said.' Even Noel Dusk was silenced for a moment.

'Mrs. Forbutt – Molly,' he said slowly and quietly after a few moments, 'thank you very much for your words. I am touched.' He paused before taking a deep breath and continuing, 'Now let me answer your earlier question…'

Before he could say anything more, Molly took hold of Arnold's hand and, looking Dusk straight in the eyes, uttered her fateful message: 'You were going to invite Arnold and me to join you on this expedition to Mars.'

Even Dusk was surprised by how forthright this seemingly acquiescent little wife could be.

'The answer is yes,' Molly continued, and Arnold nodded his head. 'You observed earlier, Noel, that Molly and I don't have that long left, so our risk is, in a way, less. My only reservation is that I am uncertain just why you should want two old codgers to join up, as it were. Surely, you need young, vigorous people on board.'

These remarks left the GreatMan almost speechless, for he had expected to have to work hard to persuade the Forbutts to come along. He was somewhat slower than usual in forming his reply.

'I had done my research on you before I invited you to Texas,' he began, 'and formed the opinion that you were rather resourceful people with a fund of common sense. Your rude remarks about Twatter, rather than disappoint or annoy me, only served to show that you were able and willing to take on anyone, however rich and powerful he – I – may be. That could have been simply because you were stupid, but I formed the opinion that you were no such thing and, that being so, that you showed a good degree of backbone and basic common sense. And that's the point, you see. Nearly everyone else selected for this adventure is on board because of his or her technical prowess. We will be a gang of experts. What we need is a modicum of colleagues whose speciality is common sense and grit. You two are the first to be selected for those reasons. I am humbled by your ready decision to accept our offer.'

'Seems everyone is making pretty speeches at the moment, mother,' Arnold said. 'An expedition like this obviously cannot hope to succeed without complete honesty from all concerned. My contribution to that, Noel – and I quite understand if this is a deal-breaker – is to tell you that Molly and I failed to catch all of the cats from whom our reputation and adventure began. Some of our friends thought we had caught them all and I didn't disabuse them, but truth to tell, we still have three young cats and one very young kitten. Molly and I love them to bits. I would like them to come with us. We would take care of them, of course. Would that be a deal breaker (DealBreaker)? For that matter, could the expedition accommodate our three and a half felines?' Molly squeezed Arnold's hand in appreciation of his unending care.

Dusk didn't even blink. Dusk hadn't got where he was without being able to make decisions quickly. 'That is perfectly okay with me, Arnold,' he replied, and continued, 'if we're all in the mood for confessions, let me admit to having done my research on you two before inviting you out here. I hired a detective over there in Australia. He is a very good detective, and he reported back to me that you do still have those four cats despite your various friends and neighbours thinking otherwise. So you see, Molly and Arnold, I am very thorough. I do my homework on everything!'

Arnold's and Molly's eyes opened rather wide. Arnold grinned.

'Well now, when can you start? Everyone on this expedition will be thoroughly trained for the next three years so that no time will be wasted once we all set foot on the Red Planet. Without being draconian about all this, the sooner you can start, the better. Naturally, from now on all your expenses will be paid by my company. I suggest that you spend the next day or so familiarising yourselves with our plans a little more, reviewing your decision – for it is obviously essential that you be really sure of it – before going home to wind up your affairs before coming out here again and then on to Mars for good. My company can assist you in any practical problems which may arise, be assured. Please explore as you will. When you're ready, contact Nancy on this number and she will help you find meals and anything else you might want to see right now. Glad to have you on board.'

Dusk departed. The Forbutts continued their tour of the exhibits, chatting to various members of Dusk's enormous team as they did, before contacting Nancy to settle their domestic arrangements for the rest of their brief stay.

Later that evening, while enjoying a decidedly splendid meal at their motel, Arnold and Molly could barely talk. For one thing, they were talked out. They had been doing little else all day and were now simply enjoying each other's company in silence. For another, their decision to embark on the last and greatest journey of their lives together was beginning to sink in.

'You know, Molly, I am still happy with our decision. I rather expected to calm down and begin to regret it, but I don't.'

'Nor me, Arnold,' Molly replied and took hold of his hand.

So there we have this picture of two, arthritic and slightly crouched oldies, holding hands as they viewed the prospect of living out their waning years millions of miles away from everyone they knew on Earth.

'We'll have the cats though, love,' Arnold said as Molly squeezed his hand.

4

They hung around at the SpaceStation and in Texas for a couple of days more before flying home. Arnold and Molly told friends of their plans. Everyone was appalled, partly at losing their friends, but mostly because they were devastated by the evident, sudden loss of their sanity. Many hours were spent in efforts to bring them to their senses. They were all wasted.

It took quite some time to dispose of all their worldly possessions, furniture, books, the sale of their beloved home. They also resolved to donate, in due course, every last cent they raised to a few relatives and a local cats' home. That should piss off a lot of people, Arnold mused. A whole life, it seemed, sent off and away. Readers, you don't wish to be bored, I am sure, with an endless repetition of their goodbyes to each and every friend and neighbour. They were all heartfelt. Everyone remained convinced that they were crackers. The whole neighbourhood was awash with tears. But finally, they left. Up, up and away on their plane back to Texas which was to become their home for the next three years or so, depending upon progress of the GreatAdventure. Snowflake, Personage, Blondie and Halfpint (who was no longer aptly named. My goodness, how they grow!) had finally been captured, loved, tamed, packed up and taken on the journey with the Forbutts. In due course, they were all assigned a small house in a purpose-built village on the perimeter of the SpaceStation.

For security and BestPractise, please understand that the house was assigned to the cats and Molly and Arnold as well.

It took less time for the cats to settle into their new home than for Molly and Arnold. Undoubtedly, the Forbutts drew on deeper wells of courage than even they had suspected, on settling into a totally new life at their age, particularly one which was to be of limited duration. It felt rather like being newlyweds all over again, in some respects.

Their main point of contact with members of Dusk's team was Nancy, the rather jolly lady who had looked after them on their first visit. It turned out that Nancy's position in the whole organisation was far more important than just being Dusk's secretary. Hers was the position of great facilitator (GreatFacilitator). She was in charge of everything other than the science, engineering or high finance. Nancy had a totally free rein to organise everything else on campus from doctors and dentists to groceries and entertainment. It also became clear that her remit was as loose as it was wide. When Arnold asked if it were possible to get free-to-air Australian TV into their little house, Nancy asked for a couple of days in which to organise it... and it was done. When Molly asked for various forms of offal – for she and Arnold were devoted to lambs' hearts, kidneys and livers and… well you don't want a full list, I'm sure – Nancy turned up trumps. And when it came to finding friends, Nancy was a star. She spent quite some time with the Forbutts so as to gauge their likes and dislikes and their tastes for company, and then arranged gatherings of a dozen or so of the locals with whom she thought Molly and Arnold might click. Nancy was very perceptive, for those evening supper and drinks parties soon yielded up three couples and two singles who seemed very much to their taste.

In each case, one partner in the couple was a technical member of the team while the other – the wife in two cases, the husband in the third – was simply the spouse with rather more time on their hands and so, perhaps, in need of more company. Or had been in need at some point in the GreatEnterprise. The singles were also spouses, but their other halves were too busy to attend Nancy's little parties at that particular time. The ethnicities of those gathered to entertain the new folk were pretty well mixed. It also turned out that their politics were mixed as well, despite Dusk's own obvious proclivities towards the right. Once again, it was apparent that Noel had no ambitions to dominate everyone's life. He was concerned with his plan to colonise Mars and nothing else was relevant to him provided it didn't get in the way. Like Arnold and Molly, themselves, everyone there understood Noel's stance and had no problems with it. That didn't prevent there being some rum folk about, as Arnold later put it to his everloving.

Take Nigel, for example. Well, you can't just take Nigel because you have to take Nigel with Clariss. While there's no doubt they're devoted to one another, they go everywhere together. That's very sweet, of course, and why shouldn't they stick like glue? But when Nigel goes off for a pee, Clariss decides she needs to find the loo as well. Arnold asked Nigel why he wanted to go to Mars and Clariss told him that it was because she did. Arnold found this reply somewhat confusing because up till that time, having observed Clariss' propensity to follow Nigel around all the time, he had assumed that Nigel was the leader, the alpha male. It turned out that Clariss was a food scientist on Dusk's team and wanted to become the person humanity would always remember as She who made Martians possible: or some such thing. Nigel adored her and followed her round like a puppy. As a reward, it seemed, Clariss allowed Nigel to lead in other matters. Like deciding when to take a pee. Mind you, Noel had chosen well, it seems, for everyone the Forbutts met spoke very highly of Clariss' reputation as a food scientist.

'Arnold's something of a foodie,' Molly offered in one conversation but garnered no response.

Then there was Sonya. Sonya was very popular.

'Particularly amongst the men,' Molly observed, 'but she never says anything.'

'Doesn't need to,' Arnold observed. Molly gave him a clip round the ear. 'Jealousy's a wonderful thing,' Arnold said.

Sonya's partner was one of Dusk's leading rocket men. Arnold asked Nancy whether he was an engineer on the rocket motors or one of the drivers.

'He means pilots,' Molly hastily interjected, giving Arnold a quick dig in his ribs. 'Can't take him anywhere.'

Nancy, bless her, lapped it all up. She had quite enough fruits in her charge not to be fazed by one more. She informed Arnold and Molly that Sonya's partner was an engineer specialising in rocket fuel manufacture from – 'Well, very little, really. He leads a team who will be in charge of the manufacture of rocket fuel on Mars, so they are very important for the return journey.'

'When might that be?' asked Arnold.

'That's not quite decided yet,' Nancy replied, 'but probably in about fifty years' time.'

'We'll not see that,' Molly replied. That was true, but Arnold looked sideways at his wife, somewhat in admiration for her sangfroid. Molly caught his glance. 'We know what we're doing,' she added.

Santoro Santini came without his wife, Pepi. She was very busy just at that time, it seemed, trying to iron out some problem with the rocket motors. Apparently, it was felt that once that particular problem was beaten, the whole drive system would be 'good to go' and the engineers would focus on various aspects of running the Martian colony itself. Santoro himself was a food scientist working on ways and means of making food production sustainable and appetising once the first colony began in earnest.

'And while we're on the journey, of course,' he added when Arnold sought to clarify his most urgent concerns, 'though we will take packets and tins of food we already know with us to help with the transition.' 'Will that include cat food?' Molly asked.

'Yes, we've been told about your cats and we are making appropriate provision for them,' Santoro assured her. So that was all right.

Molly and Arnold certainly hoped it would be all right, for it was difficult sometimes to be certain that Santoro meant what he said. He had a nervous tick in that he winked whenever he finished a sentence. Arnold asked Nancy about this after meeting Santoro for the first time and she assured him that he did mean what he said, despite this oddity.

'The thing is,' Arnold said to Molly when they were alone together, 'he even seems to wink when he hasn't actually said anything. Certainly, when he's with Sonya.'

'Maybe he winks after he's thought something,' Molly suggested, 'after all, you sometimes pull faces without saying anything in the presence of pretty girls.'

'Do I?' asked Arnold, looking decidedly puzzled.

And then there was that couple of medics who Nancy introduced them to: Wesley and Jenny Wright.

'I'm beginning to get the picture of Noel's sense of economy, 'Arnold breathed to Molly, 'Two for the price of one.' Wesley specialised in men's problems and Jenny, in women's. Both doctors, however, boasted abilities in the broadest of medical areas and could best be described as 'general specialists', however nonsensical such a description may sound.

'We're not the only medics in the party, of course,' Jenny assured the Forbutts.

'So you can always get second opinions!' Wesley continued. 'We hear you have cats,' Jenny said.

'We do animals as well,' Wesley added. 'In fact, we do the lot!' said Jenny.

'All for the price of one!' Wesley laughed.

'Except you won't have to pay!' Jenny continued. 'Not a cent,' Wesley confirmed.

Then they both laughed.

'It's like medicine in stereo,' Arnold breathed to Molly who snorted uncontrollably and then flourished a handkerchief under her nose.

'You're not sickening for something, we hope?' Wesley asked. 'No time for that,' Jenny laughed.

'Not at all,' Arnold replied as Molly said, 'Tickle', by way of explanation and snorted again.

In fairness, not all of the folk the Forbutts met at that party were "rum" as Arnold had put it. The Mishtas, for example, were an American couple of Indian ethnicity who had observed Molly and Arnold's confusion and amusement on meeting some of Dusk's band of happy warriors.

'Yes,' Pita breathed in their ear, 'there are some strange people in Noel's band of braves but most of us are fairly straightforward, I think.' Mita, her husband winked his agreement.

Molly suggested that they must all be odd in some way, 'After all, who in their right minds would join a one-way trip to Mars?'

'Not all of us will, you know,' was Pita's reply and, when Molly asked what she meant, continued, 'I should think about one half of Dusk's team will accompany him to Mars. The others, though quite devoted both to him and his plans, will remain here on Earth and form a sort of "mirror team", as it were, which will attempt to help with any problems the true Martians may encounter. Mita and I will be off to the new planet but that couple over in the corner – who are very dear friends of ours, by the way, will not.' She pointed to another Indian couple and beckoned them to meet Molly and Arnold.

It was at the third of Nancy's parties that Arnold and Molly met someone who was destined to be a key figure in this tale. Peter Handle, a lean and somewhat handsome man, probably in his late thirties, Molly supposed, was amongst those destined for the Red Planet. His role was to entertain the brave men and women who were to build humanity's greatest adventure.

'We're not likely to have much spare time to enjoy entertainment,' Arnold said, jumping straight into the first conclusion which entered his mind.

'Everybody's mind has a few neurons spare to contemplate the idiocy of this project even as he or she works his or her butt off to make it succeed,' Peter replied.

'If you feel that way, why on earth are you going with us?' asked Arnold. 'I'm not sure, Arnold,' Peter replied, 'but Dusk's magic is overwhelmingly powerful, and I understand magic.'

It turned out that Peter Handle was a magician.

'I have always admired magicians,' Arnold replied, 'but, wonderful though magic is, it's merely an entertainment, surely?'

Peter replied with some words which Arnold never forgot: 'The art of magic is to begin with gentle truth and massage, before you introduce an impossible idea which you then develop with utmost logic so that the ridiculous proposition gets forgotten under the welter of sleights of hand.' Peter smiled at Molly and Arnold, and continued, 'It's going to be my job to distract.'

'You mean, by emphasising the logic?' Arnold replied.

'Precisely.'

As Peter moved away to chat to another guest at that point, Arnold turned to Molly and said, 'I think those cats of ours would understand those sentiments, luv,' and gave her hand a squeeze. 'By gum, there are some awfully clever people around here.'

5

Arnold and Molly settled down into their Texan home quite nicely thanks to Nancy and her friends. As for the cats... well, Dusk had taken to them it seemed, for directives had been issued for a large pen to be constructed adjacent to the Forbutts' little house, large enough to give them ample space and interest but secure enough to keep them in. Well, not so much to keep them in but to keep other (wild) critters out. It seemed that Noel was as keen as the Forbutts to protect their furry friends so that they might accompany them to Mars in one piece. That is, four pieces. Of course, cats will be cats and these four were as crafty as ever and found their way out through the front of the cottage so that, after only a few weeks, they managed to find other pussycats to play with. Well, it kept them happy.

Molly and Arnold became quite close to several of those "rum folk" as the weeks passed and found enough to do to stop watching Aussie TV. Mind you, they didn't replace that with American TV, about which they had as much to say as the time they spent with the TV set switched off. The point is that their interactions with their new friends were surprisingly warm and fast developing.

They assumed that being "comrades" in the GeatEnterprise somehow accelerated and deepened their feelings for their new friends.

'They're all we've got, luv,' Arnold said to Molly one evening while they were looking back over their first couple months at the SpaceStation.

'And the cats,' Molly reminded him.

'Yes: and the cats.' Arnold replied.

It was shortly after that – just another week, in fact – that some thunderous news hit all members of the GreatAdventure. Apparently, advances made by Dusk's rocket team had ironed out the last of the problems with the motors. Tests had repeatedly gone exactly to plan, and Dusk was able to announce that the big rockets were fully operational and ready to go. More: that take-off would be in six months' time rather than after three years. Some of those destined for Mars were excited beyond all measure and just couldn't stop telling everyone again and again of their part in the enterprise. But there were some who were rather quiet. Now was the time of testing their resolve. No longer did they feel that they had the possibility of changing their minds, of sloping off, of running away. Reality had struck. Six months! It really was going to happen! Arnold and Molly took the news soberly and reasonably calmly but without any loss of resolve whatsoever. They had been quite serious when they had accepted Noel's invitation only four months earlier; they had sold up their house and possessions and said their goodbyes to all their friends back in Australia; they had known all along exactly what they were doing. The new timescale was a surprise, but it was welcome. Neither of them had that many years left, they felt, so let's get on with it while we're able. Yes, this was the first occasion in which they could play the part Noel had always held for them: to steady the ship, to keep calm and to keep others calm in this first of, no doubt, many surprises to test the expedition. And they did it instinctively. They had seen so much in their long lives that calm came to them like a river flowing into a lake.

They couldn't calm everyone, of course, if only because they hadn't met every one of the two thousand or so people on station (OnStation). But they formed a nucleus of quiet sanity amongst the brave. Noel himself certainly needed calming for he was creaming his jeans with excitement over the prospect of his life's dream coming to fruition so soon. Those who had known Dusk for years were well attuned to his passion. There was no other word for it. And now he had but six more months to wait. He called a meeting of everyone involved. He couldn't stop grinning. He was a little boy again. Apart from reiterating the revised timescale of the GreatAdventure, he had nothing to say that was at all new, but he said it anyway. In any case, much of it was new to Arnold and Molly and other bits came as confirmation of what they had gleaned from their new- found friends at Nancy's parties. Perhaps the most significant of these confirmations was that the Mars party was duplicated, in effect, so that while nine hundred people struggled on the

Red Planet's surface, a similar number copied their antics back on Earth. As difficulties arose on Mars, the nine hundred back home would re-enact their problems and so, perhaps, help to solve them. As Molly pointed out, the symmetry wasn't perfect in that while the Martian party might fear for their own lives, those back on Earth would fear for the Martians' lives. When Arnold asked her why that mattered, she replied that fear on behalf of others could be every bit as sharp as for one's self, if not more so; and that, in any case, it was different and might lead to different outcomes. Molly was showing a degree of wisdom that surprised her husband of fifty-odd years. She also added that she suspected that Noel had worked that out for himself already. Noel demonstrated another facet of his real understanding, that he had thought all this through many times already. He gave notice of a knees-up for the following evening.

'We are going to have to work especially hard during the next few months,' he said, 'so hard that it is unlikely that we'll have much energy left for a really good piss-up. Therefore, we should really push the boat out now. Nancy will let everyone know the details.'

'That is, Nancy will organise the damn thing, he means,' said Molly.

Arnold looked at Nancy with a measure of pity. Poor girl; she had so much on her plate. But no! Nancy was radiant, smiling widely and as eager as maybe to get on with so pleasant a task.

It was so like Noel Dusk to make use of every occasion in more than just one way. He announced that part of the food to be served on the morrow was to be the first large-scale run of dishes which had been especially designed for eating in space; that is to say, on the journey out. Several dishes had been designed by the famous Gaston Bloominghell in his kitchens in Berkshire, England. Nancy hastened to add that ordinary food would be available as well. Just in case, (JustInCase).

'Furthermore,' Noel added, 'Sir Daniel Attelburg will be on hand to give us all a film show of what other life forms we may encounter on Mars and on some of the problems those of us who set foot on that planet are likely to encounter so far as our own bodies are concerned.'

'In other words,' Santoro mumbled, 'as usual, Noel gives with one hand and takes with the other. This will turn out to be every bit as much a teach-in and laboratory class as a straightforward party.'

Wesley Wright quietly replied, 'Come on, Santoro: we all knew what Noel was like before we signed on!'

Someone in the crowd, who Arnold didn't recognise, whistled and cheered ecstatically. Or was that sarcastically? Regardless, it was like water off a duck's back to Dusk who heard the whistle and promptly whistled back. And then applauded. Himself, it seemed to Molly.

Snowflake was late home that evening, but Molly and Arnold were too preoccupied to notice.

***

The Forbutts began to receive an increasing number of invitations to drinks parties, lunches and dinners. It seems that the locals, who were mostly Americans, of course, found their Ossie ways quaint. Arnold couldn't help correcting their hosts by pointing out that, contrary to quite reasonable rules of pronunciation, the accepted abbreviation of Australian was pronounced as Ozzie, rather than Ossie; and further, that he and Molly were actually Poms, Brits or Limeys. He was wasting his breath, however, for no matter how often he explained it, all their American hosts could hear was Ossie, and when prodded even further, simply burst into fits of laughter and made appeals for more of the same.

'We just love your accent!' they cried.

Arnold insisted that he didn't have an accent; rather they did. They should have resented this remark, surely, but they didn't.

'Oh! Do say that again Arnold,' was all he got.

Eventually, he gave up. None of this really upset anyone, however. The Forbutts continued to be popular and their liking for their hosts only grew. Further, it seemed that there was something in the way they spoke – something more than simply their accent – which engendered confidence in those they met. The word was "down to earth", (DownToEarth).

Noel popped in on one of their little meetings one day. He didn't stay long because he was frantically busy, but he spread the love and gave renewed confidence to everyone as he dashed in and dashed out. Arnold and Molly began to feel special and to be important contributors to the cause. So did everyone else. Wesley Wright's sense of humour overflowed.

'They only need to crucify him, and he's set!' he said to Arnold and Molly behind his hand.

Nancy appeared to announce that there would be some "interesting" knickknacks (KnickKnacks?) to eat, courtesy of Gaston Bloominghell and a small team of waiters appeared with small saucers bearing goodies shaped as cubes, spheres and discs. There were some made up as spheres inside circular discs to look like Saturn.

'I hope Dusk's launching accuracy is more accurate,' observed Arnold with a smirk.

'Each to his own, pal,' Nigel, husband of food scientist, Clariss, reprimanded.

'Let's wait until we've tasted Gaston's little bites, shall we?' Arnold replied.

In fairness, the cube, the sphere, the miniature Saturn all tasted delicious and quite different from one another. What they tasted of, however, was a puzzle. 'What do you reckon, Nigel? Cube for beef, sphere for chicken?' Arnold asked.

'I don't rightly know, Arnold,' Nigel replied but continued, 'but maybe that's just as well. It means that we cannot complain that the cube doesn't taste like beef, or the crocodile of chicken.'

'Perhaps we should just say it tastes of cube?' Molly suggested.

Many around her thought that she had just about got it right. There was a hiatus in food delivery after that – though not in the liquid stuff – before Nancy announced that it was the turn of our old favourite, Huge Furry Witholdingstuff to tempt our tastebuds. Good old Huge! He presented the hungry throng with all sorts of conventional food, cooked so very well and in familiar ways. The Hominy grits were especially well liked by some of the locals. Molly and Arnold opted for a dish of lambs' kidneys with mushrooms.

'Each to her own, eh, Mather?' Arnold said quietly, not wishing to offend any of the locals.

6

That was the last big party before lift-off, but it was certainly not the last small occasion to meet up with other members of the team.

'Hey, Mather,' Arnold observed, 'it's a funny thing about prepositions, you know. The Americans play fast and loose with them, don't they? Like: get off of, and things like that. You know, using two prepositions where one will do. But what about our saying, meet up with, while the Yanks would say, meet with, which grates like hell to my ears.'

'You're too sensitive, Feyther,' Molly replied, not being in the mood for one more of Arnold's endless analyses.

Be that as it may, the Forbutts began to notice that many around them were getting increasingly jittery.

'It's only natural, luv,' Arnold said.

'Of course,' Molly replied, 'but surely they all knew exactly what they were in for long ago. After all, most of the people here had joined up long before we did.'

'Doesn't stop you getting scared, though,' Arnold observed and then a thought occurred to him. 'I wonder if these feelings convey themselves to the cats. I'd hate to think of them becoming ever more terrified as D-day approaches.

By the way, Snowflake seems to be putting on a bit of weight, don't you think?' 'It's all these parties we've been having. That's what I think. People are very kind, but I wish they'd stop slipping the cats odd morsels while they think we're not looking,' Molly replied. 'By the way, have you noticed how much they seem to like Gaston's cubes and things?'

'I hope they do,' replied Arnold, 'because I certainly noticed that several guests were only too happy to slip them off their plates. Some folk have no sense of adventure.'

It may be that the reader is dozing off a little at this point in this tale. If so, it's only fair to warn him that, for the sake of security and best practise, a big to-do is about to be related (BigToDo). It had come up to D-day minus two months at this point. A sizeable package of what we might refer to as "space gear" (SpaceGear) had been distributed to all those destined for the Red Planet. There were all the goodies in each package which you'd expect, like a spacesuit, complete with waste disposal equipment (for the use of/tested/deodorised), a small packet of personal tools comprising a torch, special screwdrivers, wrenches, aerosols and the like, special detachable intercom (sound and vision) equipment, spare batteries, battery charging equipment and goodies like that. All travellers were encouraged – well, obliged is a better word – to study all these bits and pieces.

'The phrase is "to familiarise yourself with", Arnold noted, 'There's one thing which Earthmen will take to Mars with them, for sure: red tape and verbal garbage (RedTape and VerbalGarbage).'

It should not be thought that Arnold was getting particularly crotchety as D-day approached. He was always like that. He just couldn't abide forms, other people's instructions or any form of straitjacket. Molly was only too well aware and gave him one of her sweetest smiles. In stark contrast, there were many other travellers who were only too excited about D-day and all its paraphernalia. Someone suggested that an entertainment group might form up and take to the stage dressed in their spacesuits arrayed in nets and glitter and singing to the audience through their intercoms. They were joking, of course. Dusk got to hear of the joke and thought it a great idea. Nancy was asked to arrange it all. Molly asked if Nancy was to be part of the expeditionary party. She was. There was a sharp uptick in confidence at this news for Nancy had acquired something of the status of a god. Or rather, goddess. Dusk took the role of God, of course.

Molly had a thought. 'What about the cats?' she asked, 'are they going to have their own spacesuits?'

'And just how do you think we would put them into their suits, luv?' Arnold replied. Arnold was very perceptive, as we well know. But then, he too couldn't see the way forward. 'They'll have to have something, and they'll have to be strapped in for take-off.' He thought some more for a couple of milliseconds. 'Are we supposed to hold them to our chests as we go up?' he cried, 'all four of them?'

'Or more!' added Molly.

Arnold looked sharply at her but before he could say any more, Nancy explained that they would all be placed into miniature sleeping bags attached to each other. 'They'll be like a row of pencils in a pencil case,' she explained.

'But they won't stay put for one second,' Arnold protested.

'They will, Arnold. They will be drugged, and they'll sleep through it all.'

'I wish we could be drugged, too,' Molly said.

'There'll be plenty of time for that,' replied Nancy, and moved off before they could find out what she meant.

Arnold was silent for a moment or two before he remembered Molly's remark. 'Molly, what did you mean when…'

Molly interrupted to say quite bluntly, 'Snowflake gave birth last night, luv. She has a litter of four indefinable lumps of kitten who she is licking to death as we speak.'

'Bloody hell! Here we go again.' Arnold protested, 'How…?'

'She's been out of our compound on several nights and there are plenty of other cats around, I've noticed,' Molly replied.

'I'll give her what for!' Arnold mumbled and went off to the cats' sleeping quarters, there to find Snowflake busily washing two of her minute kittens. Molly was just a step behind him. Arnold took hold of Molly's hand as he said quietly, 'They're lovely, love. She'll be a good mother, I'm sure.' Snowflake stopped grooming for a few seconds as she looked up at Molly and Arnold to give a brief miaow in appreciation of Arnold's fierce censorship.

And, for the sake of accuracy and best practise, please note the cat count had now doubled to eight.

Arnold pointed out to Molly that they must contact Nancy immediately with the news so that extra "transportation sleeping bags" could be manufactured. It never occurred to him that the new kittens could be given away to deserving families back here on Earth.

For the sake of security and greater transparency, it should be noted that Arnold's best neurons were focussed elsewhere.

Nancy came to see them after that to ask a favour. Could Molly and Arnold spend some time with Dwayne and Leera Medendy, a couple of Dusk's transform engineers who had planned to be on the Mars party but who were now in a high state of panic about the enterprise?

'Don't try to persuade them one way or another, though,' Nancy said, 'but if you can help to calm them down a little, we should be most grateful. Coming from two such sensible people as yourselves, any advice would surely be most welcome.'

'You did tell Nancy about the kittens, didn't you?' Molly remarked, after Nancy had moved on.

Arnold, of course, understood Molly's little joke only too well but suddenly thought how they might make use of it. They went in search of the Medendys who they had met briefly at one of Nancy's earlier parties. Dwayne was a lanky, skinny guy with little hair on his head but with a plentiful salt-and-pepper beard. Leera, who had rebuffed many a jibe about her monika during her life, was as short as Dwayne was not, had no beard but was blessed with a magnificent head of curly hair. When last seen by the Forbutts, they had been a very talkative couple, very engrossed in their roles which were, incidentally, to do with imaginative engineering. When asked what imaginative engineering was, they had explained that they specialised in using well-known engineering techniques in unusual circumstances. Noel Dusk had been with them on that occasion and had extolled their prowess in the field, explaining how useful they would be on Mars when the unexpected arose which was likely to be something almost every day.

'These guys are like those magicians, Pencil and Chalk,' he had enthused, 'and, boy, are we going to need our fair share of magic on this adventure!'

The Medendys' eyes were always alive and full of fun as they enthused about their latest gadget. They were the last word in lateral thinking, a disease which first came into public view sometime in the 1960s when it was identified by a guy called Pro Bono. The Medendys, that is, not their eyes.

Anyway, when Molly and Arnold found them on this occasion, they were still gabbling frantically but the fun had left those eyes. They were not describing their latest gadgets but rather, their latest feelings.

'It's all happening too quickly,' Dwayne was gabbling, 'we had expected a slow run-up to lift-off,' he was saying, 'but now it's all been sprung on us. I'm not sure we're ready to take this on. I don't want to let Noel down but, but...' He was getting just a tad hysterical as he revealed, for the hundredth time, his and Leera's fears about the expedition.

'You know, Dwayne, you and Leera don't have to stay with the travelling party. You could stay here on Earth and join the Mirror group (MirrorGroup) where your inventiveness could still be of great use to the expedition,' Arnold told him. He was quite proud of how he had papered over the crack. 'After all, if some problem arises on the Red Planet, you could try to solve it back here and send your solution to Dusk by email – or whatever electronic messaging system we're going to use. How about that? You stay here but continue in your roles as Earthbound geniuses or magicians, as you will.'

Dwayne's level of panic was such that he was about to continue on his rant when the import of Arnold's suggestion got through. Dwayne gulped air for a while as he digested what Arnold had said. Like anyone else, just because Dwayne was a near-genius in his chosen field, didn't mean he was lightning fast universally. It's a common problem. In Dwayne's case, it was a very large problem. He continued gulping down half-protestations for several more moments as the trickle down continued.

At last, he turned to Leera and explained what Arnold had suggested.

'Yes, yes, Dwayne,' Leera replied, 'but we gave our word to Noel, didn't we?'

Dwayne's countenance fell once more, hitting his boots in mere milliseconds.

Arnold saw that he must strike quickly. 'Nobody is bound to keep their word, as you call it,' he said, 'this is far too big a commitment to be left to legalistic argument. Noel, himself, understands that, and has said so to many people like yourselves who are suffering second thoughts. He wouldn't want comrades on Mars who weren't utterly convinced that they should be there; that they should be there in person. It's no shame to rethink this thing. What is important is to see how best you can serve the GreatEnterprise. You mustn't let pride get in the way of clear thinking.' Arnold was quite proud of that last remark.

Well, it seemed that Arnold had struck a chord in Leera's thinking. She suddenly felt released from the promise she imagined she had made. In her case, the penny dropped in an instant. Her eyes opened and she smiled for the first time in a week. Dwayne cottoned on shortly after that.

Arnold and Molly drifted away. Molly said, 'Well done, feyther. They'll be fine now.'

And it was true; Arnold had completely calmed the Medendys. He told Nancy what had happened. She smiled at Arnold with a modicum of gratitude. Ten days later, but without losing their joie de vivre, the Medendys announced that they would definitely be on the flight. Noel came specially to see Arnold and to congratulate him on his interpersonal skills.

'Must dash; very busy… glad to have you aboard,' he said as Arnold tried to explain what he thought he had accomplished. Arnold had assuredly lost none of his skills.

Neither had Nancy, for she appeared soon after that to present Molly and Arnold with a further "travelling bag" for the new arrivals. Talking of which – for, assuredly, the reader must be bursting with curiosity by now – the four new kittens had grown into naughty, self-propelled balls of fur. They were still unweaned but able to run around the place. Their colours? Well, one was a pale ginger with swirls all over, another was a darkish ginger with enormous whiskers, a third was an almost dark brown, rather like the brown of a Burmese and had seemingly enormous eyes, while the fourth was white, like its mother but with a distinctive golden haze when the sun shone through its fur.

'They're very handsome, Mother,' Arnold said with an obvious pride. Almost as if he'd sired them himself, Molly thought with a giggle.

Snowflake was a most attentive mother, grooming them almost non-stop, at least while they weren't suckling.

'We must think of some names, soon,' Arnold told Molly.

'Best get a vet to tell us what sex they are first, don't you think?' said Molly. Seemingly, experience was being a good teacher at last.

Wesley and Jenny Wright told them what they needed to know. The brown kitten and the white kitten were male, while the dark ginger and pale ginger ones were female. Molly thought that was a nice distribution. After days of deliberation, which in truth kept their minds off the really important future for a bit, they arrived at an agreement. The white one was to be called WhiteOne; the brown one, BrownOne; the pale ginger, PaleGinger; and the darker ginger, BigWhiskers. Arnold was pleased with the asymmetry of their choice. Molly observed in passing that they hadn't the need to know their sex after all.

'We might have need later,' Arnold observed with some perspicacity.

Relations with the cats were quite different now. Molly and Arnold had handled the kittens from the beginning and Snowflake had raised no objections, so that now these lovely little furballs climbed all over them both. PaleGinger was in the habit of running up Molly's arm, turning around until she was back near her elbow, at which point, she curled up and fell instantly asleep. She melted Molly's heart every time. BrownOne would climb into Arnold's hand, stay standing and peer deeply into Arnold's face.

'Aye, Mother,' was all Arnold could say.

Snowflake herself appeared to be learning a few interpersonal skills from her offspring for she too began to interact more closely with both Arnold and Molly than she ever did. Just little things, like the occasional lick of the hand or the twirl around the ankles. Blondie, as auntie, took to the newbies like a duck to water, and generally speaking the quantity of love spread by all around increased enormously.

7

There were but two weeks to go before lift-off and Noel Dusk had called a meeting of everyone in his teams: those who would toddle off to Mars with him, and those MirrorMen (and women) who would back them up. Altogether, there were about eighteen hundred people assembled in the great hall (GreatHall) in front of a stage upon which the GreatMan sat. Actually, the great hall was simply a large section of one of the rocket assembly bays in the great factory (GreatFactory). Dusk had asked Nancy to organise it all. Dusk rose to speak.

'Well,' he began in jaunty style, 'we're very nearly there. Not on Mars, of course, but at lift-off. I am incredibly proud to say that barely ten team members who signed on to make the trip have re-thought their options. Nevertheless, they have graciously agreed to join our mirror team, so their expertise will not be lost. It is entirely understandable to me that some folk should feel unable to go through with this great but dangerous adventure, to help establish an outpost for mankind on a distant planet, especially when technology is yet at a tender stage for such an undertaking. We have all heard the nay-sayers' (NaySayers') view that the time is not yet ripe

(NotYetRipe). Perhaps they are right, but I have more than a suspicion that for such people, the time would never be right. Anyway, I think the time is now ripe and, like all of you, I am putting my life and fortune where my mouth is.'

'Pretty big mouth!' could be heard from the body of the hall.

Dusk laughed with everyone else. Unfazed, he continued his address: 'You have all been given a large e-book containing every last detail of this whole enterprise, from take-off, to the journey there, to setting up on Mars after we arrive. If you have read every word, well done! The detail is there in full so that anyone can find, I hope, the answer to any question which might arise. It is not there as some form of compulsory reading. We all have our parts to play, some more technical than others, and there is no necessity for everyone to know everyone else's tasks in any more detail than simple curiosity demands.

'During the twenty-four hours before lift-off, those taking the trip will be settled into their places for lift-off. They will be helped to strap in, as it were,' Dusk broke off and sought the eyes of Molly and Arnold in the crowd, 'including those lovely cats which so many have met in the past months – and, by the way, Snowflake has given birth to four kittens, in case some of you weren't aware…'

'I didn't know he knew that, luv,' Arnold murmured to Molly. 'Noel knows everything,' she replied.

'For those who may have an interest, by the way, the cats carry bag is rather like an oversize flexible cigar case with one pouch for each animal. Now, as you know, our expeditionary force comprises five separate big rockets, so there will be roughly three hundred of us in each of three ships. The plan is for these three rockets to take off within five minutes of one another. Shortly afterwards, the two remaining ships, carrying supplies of various kinds, will follow us all. The passenger-bearing sections will separate from the main power and fuel sections after the primary burn and the large fuel tanks and motor sections will return to base for re-use in the manner we have become famous for. However, we have made modifications to the upper passenger sections on those three vessels so as to allow a secondary degree of acceleration as we leave the Earth's gravitational pull. Separation will not be made with the two remaining rockets for our intention is to guide these ships to Mars intact so that we will have available both rocket engines for future use and large empty fuel tanks for conversion into our first habitation on the surface of the Red Planet. We have tested the procedures already and I am perfectly confident that everything will go smoothly. The first few minutes' flight will be rather uncomfortable for the acceleration will be…'

'Something else,' Arnold remarked, sufficiently loudly to raise a few smirks from those in his immediate vicinity.

'…but after that,' Dusk continued, 'our trip should be altogether enjoyable. Should you feel compelled to shout out or make other negative commentary in that early phase of lift-off, feel free because everyone will be wearing headgear and the intercom will be turned off for that stage.

There will follow a period of further but gentler acceleration even after we leave Earth's orbit. This is somewhat different to what had been planned when our departure was scheduled to be three years away. The reason is that that later departure had been chosen to optimise the window for the shortest overall travel time to the Red Planet. Our earlier departure means that the journey will be much further. Further in distance, but because of our redesigned acceleration and special trajectories, it should not be too much longer in time. Altogether, we expect to arrive in Mars' orbit in about seven months.

Now seven months is a long time to stay cooped up in our rockets. They have been designed to transport three hundred people apiece in modest comfort but, even so, it won't be like Arthur C. Clark's 2001 Odyssey and that great wheel (GreatWheel?). So the plan is for us to enjoy the experience of space travel for about two weeks at each end of the journey – departing Earth and arriving at Mars – but for us to sleep the rest of the way. Our medical experts have developed a means of keeping us all in hibernation for the six months in the middle of our journey – including the cats, Molly and Arnold…' Noel raised his voice as he looked out at the Forbutts, continuing, '– which involves sleep-inducing drugs and some rather clever cryogenics. Once again, for those with a high degree of curiosity, the great book (GreatBook) provides some rather detailed descriptions of the whole process.'

'Maybe reading the book could be substituted for taking the sleeping pills,' some wag from the middle of the hall suggested.

Dusk continued: 'Each of the three passenger vessels will carry more than enough food to keep us satisfied during the journey so everything up to the moment of landing is very well catered for. It is planned that all five vessels should land on Mars within one hundred metres of one another in a depressed area, a kind of wide ravine, fairly near to the South Pole. Once we land, and the dust settles, literally, we can make our first extravehicular walk, as the pioneering astronauts used to have to say. We, however, will simply go outside. Initially, the plan is for us to continue to live and sleep in our travelling compartments but, as soon as we are able, we shall unpack material from the fourth and fifth rockets and begin to convert the empty shells into more permanent and spacious homes, homes which we anticipate will have to last us for a couple of decades – that is, Earth decades – at least. We cannot be precise about things like that, of course, because there will be much to learn, and we shall have to extemporise. That, of course, is where the mirror group will come into its own, providing a separate set of brains and ideas together with the full gamut of Earth's facilities to help us. I expect that we will make ever more use of our Earthbound colleagues as the years tick on. I also expect that we will begin to grow much of our own food and begin the task of synthesising fuel for a return journey in, maybe, fifty years. Many of us will not make that journey. All of us will experience fear, loneliness and sadness from time to time. But then so we might back here on Earth. What we shall experience, which those remaining will not, is the exhilaration of being amongst the world's greatest explorers in history, of being the first men and women – and cats, Molly and Arnold – on man's second planet. Our names will live forever more.'

'It's going to be difficult for those following us to remember nine hundred names!' Clariss shouted from the floor to much mumbled agreement and laughter. 'That's true,' Dusk replied, 'and it is also true that my name will be the one uniquely remembered. That is inevitable.'

Noel was interrupted again from the floor. 'You have been the one to set this whole thing going, Noel. Nobody can object to your name being to the fore!' Before either Molly or Arnold could identify the speaker, there arose a wave of applause from everyone in the room. It went on for several minutes. Noel Dusk was very much moved. As were we all.

Dusk continued: 'In rockets four and five, we shall carry all manner of tools, including metal-forming gear so that we can build our long-term quarters, hopefully in whatever style we find most useful and appealing, for whatever reason. There will be many seeds and much food-cultivation material so that we can get started on self-sustainability straight away. There will also be a couple of small hovercraft we can use to explore the surrounding geography. And many, many batteries.'

'Of course!' Santoro Santini shouted sardonically, to much mirth from those who caught what he said.

'Shit!' another member of the audience called out.

'Ah, yes! Thank you for reminding me,' Dusk replied with his boyish grin. 'Waste disposal is something which will concern us all from the moment of take-off. Appropriate facilities are provided and, unlike the very cramped conditions which space travellers had to suffer in the twentieth century, ours have a more than acceptable degree of dignity. All human body waste – and cat waste, but you will have to make arrangements, as we have discussed, Molly and Arnold – will be collected and processed into potable water and odourless manure to aid our gardening projects. Once again, the whole process has been tested in great detail and works perfectly. The toilets as used on the flight are complex affairs, of course, because of the absence of gravity. Once we land on Mars, however, our toilets will be rather like those on Earth, albeit with some clever gains in efficiency. Once more, full details for those of an enquiring mind are to be found in the GreatBook. I don't think I need to describe more details right now.'

'I'll drink to that!' came a shout from the floor.

'That reminds me,' Dusk replied, 'those who are regular drinkers have been warned already, but I need to restate the position. Alcohol will be in short supply for the foreseeable future. Not for religious reasons, with or without a capital R, but simply because we have to pare down weight in our travel baggage. I have no intention of creating a nanny state. We are all adults and must make our own decisions, but we can only do that within the practical constraints our voyage imposes upon us. Accordingly, it has been decided that some booze will be available while we're awake on the journey but only on a couple of occasions when we might want to make toasts to our past and future lives. Once we get established on Mars, there is no reason why we should not set up stills and other equipment to manufacture alcohol but, of course, such endeavours must take their turn with all the other tasks which will arise. So I expect it will be some time before we can get smashed on a regular basis. You never know, by the time we can establish a plentiful liquor supply, we might have lost the taste for it!'

'Can pigs fly on Mars? Anybody know?' came a call from the body of the hall, to much merriment.

'Entertainment, however,' Dusk continued, 'will be in plentiful supply for it will all be stored electronically, of course, and be available to all on demand. Music, films, good stuff, rubbish, all of it. I have no wish to act as censor. Once again, we are all grown-ups, and we can amuse ourselves in that way however we wish. On the other hand, we will follow most of the laws of America and the civilized world in general. In time, we may decide to add to, subtract from, or to alter any or all of these inherited, "Earth" laws but, until we do, we'll stick with what we already have. I wouldn't worry too much about fancy laws about trespass or slander, mind you, because we do not have any lawyers within our midst to feed on the attendant litigation. I dare say, however, that such skeins of civilization will arise in due course, quite likely around the time that alcohol becomes endemic once more. Look, I'm no lawyer or social scientist but I am a cynic and a realist. I know only too well that neither I nor any other human being in our new society will have the power to prevent the re-emergence of the world's peccadillos. I most sincerely do hope, however, that we will manage to put in place laws and, if necessary, physical restrictions, to prevent the worst atrocities of mankind. Those will not be something, however, which I will seek to impose.

'We will have some telling times ahead of us, ladies and gentlemen. I know that many of you have thought a lot about all that, already. We shall just have to find our way through it all in due course. Till then, while we are just too busy to think rationally about such things, we'll live according to the standards with which we are already acquainted.

'I have just a couple more things to say. One is that all minute details of what each of us must do during our remaining days are documented in the GreatBook. Nancy, who is part of the travelling party, by the way...' Noel was interrupted by a great whoop of joy from the hall, followed by rapturous applause and foot stamping. Nancy beamed wider than most people have faces. Dusk continued: 'I just wanted to say, that our beloved Nancy will be around to help anyone struggling with all that.

'And finally, without going on too long about it I hope, I want to thank each and every one of you for your participation in this great adventure and for your courage. It is an honour to fly with you. We are about to make history, ladies and gentlemen. Records of our deeds will last for evermore. We are about to taste glory! Bon voyage!'

Nancy had just received very warm applause. Noel Dusk's was dramatic. He was accorded a standing ovation of more than quarter of an hour. He tried to dampen it down, but nobody was having any of that. The hero worship was amazing. It was a day to remember indeed.

Afterwards, Arnold remarked to Molly, 'We should have given ourselves a standing ovation too, you know.' Molly smiled and hugged him. The cats came in for special attention that evening too: salmon with all the trimmings. 'I can't help thinking that it's wrong for us to take them with us, luv,' Arnold said, 'but I can't bear to part with them either.'

'We'll look after them very carefully,' Molly replied. The cats seemed to sense that something was special that day. But that could just have been Molly and Arnold's imagination, of course. Or the salmon.

8

Take-off for Molly and Arnold's spaceship was just five minutes away. Theirs was the second rocket scheduled to go. The first one, half a mile or so away, had gone off with a great deal of noise, flame and smoke but none of the passengers in any of the rocket ships heard or saw a thing. That take-off had been entirely successful. Everything had gone to plan. They knew that because mission control had said so. But mission control's voices were all they heard through their noise-cancelling headphones. Each passenger was very well strapped into his and her seat and, in Molly's and Arnold's cases, each of them cuddled a large package of four oversized cigars held tight within a specially fashioned protective spacesuit. The sedated pussycats were completely out of it. Arnold, for one certainly, rather wished he was out of it, too. He was so scared, but his body surprised him by not reacting to fear as he had feared. No, he did not wet himself – or worse. It seemed as if every system in his body was so pursed up that nothing presented itself but pure, liquid fear. He just held Molly's hand. Otherwise, each had to experience the fear individually.

Mission control had begun the countdown some time earlier. They were now down to the last twenty seconds. Even in that short window, Arnold managed to imagine himself calling out, 'Hang on a minute. I'm getting off!' which was probably a good thing. It kept him occupied for a few seconds. He heard the words, "Lift- off," just milliseconds before he felt a great shuddering. He didn't really hear those rocket engines, but he sure felt them. The push in his back was far, far less than he had expected. 'This is going to be a doddle!' he thought. The thought didn't last too long before that push noticeably increased.

And increased. And yet more and yet more. During the next few minutes, he experienced the most terrifying acceleration; his head would surely explode. The spaceship was shuddering itself to pieces. It would certainly explode before his head. Thank God! It would all be over soon. But it wasn't. It got worse and worse. Oh God! Please let this end, he wanted to shout. But he couldn't move his face or his lips, or his tongue. He wanted to look at Molly to see how she was coping but he couldn't turn his head, not even by one degree. We should never have signed up for this. Give us our money back!

Quite suddenly, the shuddering ceased. Same with the acceleration. He became conscious of some gabbling in his headset, something about "Launch complete; launch successful!" Now he could turn his head, with some difficulty to be sure because of muscles which were still tight from fear. His eyes met Molly's and they both teared up at the same time. He managed to reach across and kiss her. There came a lot of gabbling in his earphones. All about altitude, time from lift-off, time to Earth orbit, details of how exactly to plan their trajectory. Arnold was more than content to leave all that to the whizzkids back at mission control. He wished he could see out of a window but there wasn't one. Later into the journey, scenery from external cameras would play onto screens inside the ship and they had been promised wonderful views. But, for now, there was just about nothing to see. At least, he was comfortable again. There was no sensation of movement at all, although he knew that they were travelling at many thousands of kilometres an hour. It was so smooth. If it hadn't been for the seemingly incessant gabbling in his headphones, it would have been even smoother.

'For the sake of security and best practise,' the voice was saying, 'please stay exactly as you are for the next few minutes. You will be instructed further, shortly.'

Some minutes later, an excited announcement came from Noel Dusk: 'All five spaceships have launched successfully; every little thing has gone exactly as planned. We're on our way. Please wait for further instructions.'

'Easy-peasy, piece of cake,' Arnold said to friends across the aisle, 'we could do that every day!' Then he felt stupid for making such a childish remark. He needn't have worried. Nobody heard because all headphones were exclusively connected to mission control. Arnold got a grip. 'We're on our way,' he said to his non-existent audience.

'Too right, mate!' someone replied. The intercom had been switched on. Arnold wanted to speak to Molly but didn't quite know how.

The flight captain came on: 'Well done, everybody. Hopefully, the worst part of our journey is over. But keep your seat belts fastened until advised otherwise. From now on, your experiences will be something like those you have had on aeroplanes.'

'God! I hope not,' someone from across the aisle said.

Arnold was able to take Molly's hand and look into her face. He had forgotten just how beautiful her eyes were. He hugged her closely.

'I hope we're doing the right thing, Molly,' he said.

Molly, ever the wiser of the pair, replied, 'A fine time to ask that question, luv.'

'How are the cats?' Arnold asked.

They looked inside the cats' cigar boxes. Everything seemed just as before take-off. They were well out of it all and wouldn't be woken for another day yet. Shortly after that, their video screens, on the backs of the seats in front of them, lit up and they were able at last to see the view outside. The cabin lights were dimmed to help them distinguish one speck of light from another in the vast blackness. Their camera swung backwards for a view of what lay behind and there it was! That beautiful blue and white orb they knew as home. They had no sensation of movement, so it was impossible to tell whether they were leaving Earth or moving toward it. They knew, however, that it was the former. The camera panned about and found a relatively bright speck to their rear and zoomed in on it. It was rocket ship number three and a light set into its nose blinked steadily at them. The camera panned a little to one side and zoomed further, this time to identify the fourth vessel. After some moments, whoever was operating the system found the fifth vessel even further back. Then the camera swung round to point in front of their ship and showed a clear picture of the back end of spaceship number one with an array of five engines. Those engines, like those on their own vessel and on the one immediately behind, had been added some months ago in order that extra thrust could shortly modify their trajectory and accelerate them again – though less violently – so as to catch up onto an optimum course to Mars. Altogether, thought Arnold, we are rather like an armada of Vasco da Gama or of Christopher Columbus, our line-up of five ships bravely bound for a new land, or planet in this case, sailing slowly on: or, once again in this case, bloody quickly.

The camera operator then gave views elsewhere by panning slowly around. The views were breathtakingly beautiful. Arnold and Molly had seen the Milky Way from a couple of "outback" sites in Australia where light pollution from Earth's civilization was minimal and had almost suffered religious conversion on the spot, but this was way beyond all that. It wasn't black out there. Rather, it was a blaze of glory.

Molly said, 'I can't wait to be on Mars where we shall be able to look up at any time and see all this any time we want.'

'It will confuse the cats, I reckon,' Arnold replied, ever the one to look ahead at things.

The ship's captain came on their headphones. 'We plan to have the first of three extra burns before shutting everything down for five months, as you know. The first of these will be in six hours' time so feel free to move around and meanwhile, we shall be serving a meal. I guess some of us will be ready for it after fasting in preparation for our take-off. And, just to reinforce mission control's messages, everything has gone exactly to plan and there are no issues to report.'

'Or to hide!' one humourist a few rows away from the Forbutts added. 'You know, Mother, he's just the sort of reason I never subscribed to Face off and Twatter.'

Molly had heard it all before. 'Yes, feyther,' she replied in her very best voice of the long-suffering.

The time had come for the first major adventure of their adventure. They were about to unbuckle and leave their seats so that they could "stretch their legs" and talk to friends several rows away from them. The adventure arose from the fact that they were in a gravity-free environment. Like everyone and his wife, they had seen countless videos of astronauts floating around in the gravity-free home of the Space Station, for example. Now they were going to experience it for themselves inside a vessel which bore many similarities to the inside of a commercial airliner. Arnold was really looking forward to all this.

'Come on, Mother,' he said, 'let's go for a swim.'

As they released their tethers, and gave just a little push on their armrests, they gradually, smoothly, magically began to float along in mid-air. Arnold tried flapping his legs to gain some degree of control but to no avail. They had begun to float along, and they would clearly continue exactly like that until they hit something which would bring them to a stop. Then Arnold noticed several ceiling straps and, being the sharp fellow he was, realised what they were for. He reached out and grabbed one of the straps and came to a halt. At least his arm came to a halt. The rest of his body continued to sail along until his arm pulled it back: by which time, he was now upside down – whatever that meant in the absence of gravity, he thought, for, as we well know, Arnold was a sharp thinking, incisive machine. Meanwhile, Molly had grabbed hold of her husband's leg so putting further strain on his arm holding onto the strap.

Arnold called out to a man in a seat some couple of yards further on: 'Look out, Harry! We're on our way,' whereupon he very gently launched himself and Molly towards said Harry's seat, reaching out to take hold of the grab handle there ('Good idea to put those handles everywhere,' Arnold thought). They arrived almost gracefully, being the quick learners they were, turning over so as to be able to chat to Harry and his wife, Penny, in a more-or-less conventional mode.

'I could get to like this, Harry,' Arnold remarked, grinning widely, and then he asked Harry how he had fared throughout the rest of the journey so far, the answer to which kept the four of them happy for well over half an hour.

Meanwhile, many others had left their seats to experience the joys of weightlessness. Some had learned almost instantaneously how to perform somersaults, how to bounce off seat backs and the ceiling, how to land on their hands. Everyone had become a kid again.

The captain's voice came on the speakers: 'Do be careful, folks! I know it's fun and all that. But we don't want any broken bones out here. We can cope with them if we have to, of course, but it will be far easier to attend to such things in the gravity of Mars than in the weightlessness here.'

Somebody down the lounge remarked, 'Yes, Daddy,' which garnered a sprinkling of laughter around the place.

'Even so,' thought Arnold, He's right. We should take care.' Good old Arnold.

They left Harry and Penny, "stretched their legs" and chatted with several other fellow adventurers. Everybody was more than a little delirious, having come down from their individual peaks of fear and terror to the even plains of self-satisfaction and soporific relief. By and large there were few attempts at childish jokes. Relief and quiet pride guided their demeanour. A somewhat different response came when their meals arrived. These were their first of very many examples of engineered food. They were small in size, tasted quite good but of exactly what, no-one knew, were light in weight (more correctly, were of no weight at all, of course, but of small mass) but, surprisingly, were quite satisfying. Gaston Bloominghell or someone had done a good job. To the surprise of many on board, the food was served with a container of quite reasonable Chablis, which took a little practise to suck from. Somehow, their earliest of moments in life came to the fore once more, and they managed. The fact that they were trying to get at alcohol probably helped their efforts. This meal was clearly of some significance.

There were clock faces adjacent to everyone's screen on which the time was given as from Earth lift-off. Arnold saw it register as 000:04:34. That meant no days, plus four hours and thirty-four minutes since leaving Texas. It seemed a damn sight longer to Arnold but, for the sake of safety and peace of mind, it cannot be stressed too strongly that that clock, like everything else on these vessels, was as accurate and reliable as everything else Noel Dusk had turned his mind to.

Talking about our Noel, the reader might well be perplexed about the great man leaving behind all his other businesses, battery manufacture, solar panels, electric cars, low altitude Earth communications satellites, and all the rest. Please don't fret. Noel had all that organised. He planned to manage and develop all these enterprises from Mars. Okay, so he wouldn't be around to slap people across their heads if they tried to cheat him or such like, but he had an army of lawyers and his hands on the purse strings. So, for the sake of security and your peace of mind, rest assured that Noel Dusk had got it all sewn up. No worries.

Time passed ever so quickly and soon there came an announcement that everyone should resume their seats and strap themselves in securely. Attendants would be passing through to make sure all was well, after which there would be the first correctional burn which would last for a full five minutes. The acceleration would be more than noticeable but nothing like lift-off. On their screens they would be able to see the view ahead of them and watch ship number one fire its first burn, twenty seconds before theirs. And there it was: suddenly a blaze of orange light from number one's engines, followed immediately by the sight of that rocket rapidly diminishing in size. Barely had Arnold, Molly and all their companions registered that fact, when they felt rumblings aft, followed by a considerable push in their backs. No, it certainly was not like lift-off, but it was a very strong push, nevertheless. And it went on for longer. The view of the rear of number one ship became larger and, by the time its engines had ceased firing, it seemed almost as large as when they had first seen it. Seconds later, their own engines stopped firing, the push ceased immediately, and peace reigned once more. Arnold turned to Molly and smiled, this time without strain. They were getting to be old hands at all this.

The views sideways shown on their screens looked exactly as they had before but when they were shown the rear view, the Earth was considerably smaller now. Still the largest thing around (they didn't look at the sun) and still obviously blue and white but it was obvious that they had moved on quite a way.

The ship's captain came on the speakers: 'That all went perfectly to plan. I have reports that the same goes for our leading ship and for the third passenger ship, too. We should get reports about our two resources vessels soon. I will let you know in due course. Meanwhile, feel free to wander around and chat to your fellows. The next burn will be in twenty hours, so I suggest that you think about sleep in, say, four hours' time. Obviously, it's up to you.'

Arnold observed that it was somewhat restricting that they could only watch what was offered on screen. A system's engineer across the aisle put him right, explaining that he was watching the default channel, showing him how to select another channel on which he could rotate a camera as he liked.

'Good grief!' observed Arnold, 'Does that mean there are more than three hundred cameras out there so that everyone can look at anything they want all at the same time?'

'Not to worry, Arnold,' he was told with a somewhat wan smile, 'electronic sampling takes care of it all. It only seems as if you have a camera all to yourself.' 'Oh!' Arnold replied and said no more, for Arnold was a sharp fellow and he knew immediately when he was out of his depth. He looked across at Molly and rolled his eyes. 'Clever,' he mumbled as he began to play with his screen manipulator buttons. 'I wonder if there are any other channels,' he said, half to himself, and began to explore. In no time, up came *I love Lucy*. 'Seen it,' he mumbled and went in search of more. By the time he had trawled through twenty or so American TV channels – or recordings thereof: he wasn't sure which – he went back to the main channel and thought he might talk to his wife instead. American TV can have that effect.

Arnold and Molly thought that they would follow the captain's advice and made themselves comfortable for their first sleep. Although there were some three hundred people on board – plus eight cats – together with considerable supplies of food, water and tools, there was quite enough room for everyone's seat to form a bed.

'Just like business class, luv,' Arnold said, approvingly as they snuggled down, 'but without the roar of engines,' for there was ever-increasing silence as their fellow passengers also prepared for sleep. In any case, they all had noise-cancelling headphones if they wished to use them. Some folk, of course, can't get to sleep in perfect silence particularly city-slickers.

***

Music played quietly and then a little less so. Arnold began to stir. Some folk a couple of rows behind were snoring rather too loudly for his taste. The captain's voice came over the intercom:

'Good morning, ladies and gentlemen. Breakfast will be served in twenty minutes' time. Enjoy the view. Earth has diminished noticeably.'

Yes, it had. Arnold began to understand in a visceral way that they really had left home. For good. It was, quite literally, an awful moment. He nudged Molly who was still in the land of nod.

'We've really left Earth, luv,' he said quietly. Molly mumbled something incomprehensible.

'Time to wake up, luv. Breakfast,' he said as he adjusted his seat into a sitting position. He checked the cats. They were still fast asleep, as planned. In due course, the captain announced that the second burn would take place in two hours and that they would be given twenty minutes warning to sort themselves out and strap in. It would last for the same time as the first correctional burn and acceleration would be more or less the same. And so it was. An announcement came some moments after the burn that all was well; indeed, that every little thing had gone exactly to plan for all five rockets. And, finally, that there would be just one more burn, in twelve hours, after which everybody might care to enjoy the view for a week or more before the big sleep (BigSleep). They would be given ample warning of that.

A number of café areas had been set aside within the large passenger pod so that people might take a break and meet up with friends to compare notes in greater comfort than was to be had simply by hanging onto handles on seat backs.

Much later, a voice came over the intercom: 'Ladies and gentlemen, for the sake of safety and best practise, we suggest that you buckle in when you take a seat in a café area.' They were also informed that the third and last burn would be made in roughly five hours' time so would they all please be in their seats well before then. They were and the burn happened more or less as before, was followed by a self-satisfied announcement that all had gone exactly to plan for their rocket and for all the rest also.

'Just like shelling peas, luv,' our super-relaxed superhero observed. It was. No one could deny Dusk his glory. Everything was absolutely tickety-boo. Arnold had a quick look back at Earth. There it still was, still blue, or rather bluish now, but considerably smaller. They were advised to get some sleep soon so that several tasks could be practised on the morrow.

Soon after breakfast, Wesley and Jenny Wright came to the Forbutts. 'Time to awaken those little fur balls of yours,' Jenny said but, to Molly's great surprise, Arnold stayed Jenny's hand.

'Look here, Jenny, no one could want to see and hear our cats out and about again, so why are we awakening them? Why not let them sleep all the way to Mars?'

'We could do that, Arnold, but we thought it would be good to see that all was well, that our hibernation techniques are going as they should, and…' Jenny hesitated a moment, smiled kindly, and continued, 'wouldn't it be nice for them to experience the joys of weightlessness as well?'

Arnold saw Jenny's wet eye before replying, 'You are a softee, aren't you, Jenny?'

Molly was far more practical. 'What if they want to go to the toilet?' she asked, 'Floating over everyone's heads and pooing wouldn't be nice!'

'Ah!' Arnold replied, 'It wouldn't fall, luv. There's no gravity!' 'It wouldn't be nice to see, though,' Molly persisted.

Wesley came to the rescue: 'We are all going to have to get used to all sorts of new things in our new lives, Molly. I guess we can take it'.

'In any case,' Jenny broke in, 'one of the side effects of our sleeping draughts is to diminish the urge to urinate or to defecate.'

Which is just as well, really, because Arnold was a little disingenuous about the poo not falling because it would, of course, be expelled and so have a velocity of its own. Arnold could be ruthlessly logical at times.

'Your honesty does you credit, Wesley,' Molly replied, 'but you lack something in sensitivity.'

'All right, you two: wake them up,' Arnold said, 'Will it take long for them to come out of hibernation?'

'Just seconds before they regain all their faculties,' Jenny replied as she introduced a small vial of gas into the cats' cigar boxes. And boy! Was she right! All eight of them began to stir more or less at the same time. Jenny opened their cigar box, and Arnold and Molly were greeted by the most beautiful orchestration of purrs they had ever known. It was almost as if the cats were saying, "About time, too!"

Arnold reached out to pick up Snowflake who he passed on to Molly, and then Blondie to whom he gave a gentle kiss. Very carefully, he let go of Blondie who tried to jump onto his shoulder but, having no purchase on the pure air around her, just remained where she was with her legs reaching out ineffectively. There are those who say that cats don't make facial expressions. Well, nuts! The look of surprise and consternation on Blondie's face was a hoot. Arnold reached out and took her back and cuddled her and assured her that everything was all right, that we are here to love you, and… and all that sort of soppy stuff. But now Personage and Halfpint and the four newbies were beginning to ask for cuddles too, and to get out of their places in the cigar box. Arnold lifted them out one by one and placed them gently in mid-air, side-by-side. The Forbutts' companions from several rows of seats away turned round to look at this feline display. Each cat and kitten was turning its head this way and that, occasionally miaowing, but mostly purring. Arnold took Blondie's front paws and held them onto Snowflake's tail, in turn attached Personage's paws to Blondie's tail, Halfpint to Personage, WhiteOne to Halfpint, BrownOne to WhiteOne, PaleGinger to BrownOne, BigWhiskers to PaleGinger, and finally, Snowflake to BigWhiskers, so forming a circle of eight cats. He gave the circle a very gentle shove so that it began to rotate: Slowly. majestically, miaowfully, purringly. The noise of eight rotating pussycats purring for all they were worth was as deafening as it was delightful. Someone called out for a microphone so that everyone on the spaceship could hear this wonderful sound. Then Santoro Santini called out: 'Alexa! Play *Blue Danube*,' and the strains of that lovely waltz filled the cabin. Arnold hadn't even been aware that the cabin was blessed (cursed?) with Alexa's munificence. Molly hadn't even heard of it. But there it was: a circle of eight, colourful cats, holding onto each other as they slowly revolved to the sound of Johann Strauss's lovely music. *Space Odyssey 2001*, eat your heart out! Snowflake let go of Big Whisker's tail and the whole thing began to unravel. Arnold had to reach up and take hold of as many of the cats as he could before they bumped into things or flew off down the cabin. Molly, too, scrambled to catch their charges. Even Jenny had to join in the recovery.

'We brought something along for just this eventuality,' she told Molly, and produced eight carry-bags, each with transparent plastic windows at each end which could be fastened with strips of Velcro. They put the cats into these little bags which had a sort of protective bubble-wrap on the outside and then Jenny told Arnold that they could now safely let the cats explore the cabin.

'Just give their bags a very gentle push and they will float off down the cabin where you may be sure that there will be many other passengers who will enjoy their company for a while. They won't get lost!'

Arnold was rather concerned about how the cats would take to all this, but he needn't have worried. They adored it. And so did the people they met along the way, some of whom the cats had already met back on Earth and, in some cases at least, they met folk who remembered their names. Pretty well wherever those cats went, they promoted cries of love and joy. They brought about such feelings of relief from the strains which the space-trip had brought forth – and still did – that many of the space-travellers were brought to tears. And laughter.

After about an hour of catmania, Jenny sent forth a call for their return: 'It's almost time for the little darlings to toilet,' she announced on the intercom, 'and I'm sure nobody wants to deal with that, so please send them back so we can attend to it.' By now, the cats were completely familiar with space travel, that is to say, with travelling through the air in straight lines, so that passengers were able to project the little darlings back home at much more adventurous velocities than they had experienced when getting their little space legs. From behind them, from in front, all eight cats smoothly sailed back to Arnold and Molly whose fame, incidentally, had by now grown enormously. Jenny led the Forbutts to a special area away from the passenger seating in which was a large litter tray under cover of a partially transparent plastic sheet. When all eight cats were inside, Jenny turned a switch which produced a gentle airflow within the litter box so that the cats could poo in peace, leaving the humans in comfort. Things had been planned beautifully. Arnold was quite amazed at how much thought and effort had gone into such mundane details.

It was much later, when Noel Dusk came on Arnold's and Molly's screens to tell them how, from the lead rocket, he had seen and heard the "cat rotor" together with the *Blue Danube* waltz and the subsequent reactions of other passengers.

'Now, I hope, you can see why I was so keen for you and Molly to bring your cats on this adventure. Most other team members are here for one technical reason or another, or to accompany a spouse who is so engaged. Your purpose, and that of your feline charges, is to spread happiness and to reset sanity when needed. And I am sure there will be many occasions when your subtle guidance will be sorely needed. I only hope that the rest of us can attend to *your* needs when required. Enjoy the rest of the trip. Isn't it amazing so far?' Dusk was grinning from ear to ear. His lifelong ambition was under way (UnderWay).

It was about a week or so later (Arnold was losing track of time despite the space clock on the seat-back in front of him) when the announcement came that preparations for the big sleep (BigSleep) were about to be made. Everyone would strap in and, when instructed, take the special sleeping draught, which was actually the same as that which had been given to the cats but larger. Everyone's vital signs would be monitored so that it would be certain that each and everyone's (the latter word was emphasised) deep sleep was established and monitored. Only then would the heating in each spaceship be cut and replaced slowly and gradually with a marked degree of cooling. They wouldn't actually be in deep freeze, in case anyone was worried, for that would cause some irreversible tissue damage, but they would be far colder than normal levels of comfort would tolerate. The whole procedure had been thoroughly tested on Earth many times without a single problem arising. Everyone might sleep peacefully.

'Rest in peace!' some wag from three rows back could be heard quite clearly.

After some six months, the whole process would be slowly reversed. Only when temperatures were all back to normal would a whiff of "wake-up gas" be administered and some minutes later, we'd all be back to normal.

I wonder what our dreams will be like, Arnold mused for he was well used to dreaming. He and Molly embraced for the umpteenth time on that strange journey, strapped in, and waited. Attendants came round to distribute the knockout pills and much later an announcement came to the effect that all seat belts were now recorded as well fastened. The cats had already been put into sleep mode and were well protected in their cigar box. Everyone was instructed to take their pills, and everybody did so.

9

'Wake up, ladies and gentlemen, wake up!' came a voice over the intercom. Not very loudly, more of a gentle, almost soothing voice. Actually, it was rather boring – or was it bored? No, it was artificial, Arnold realised. It was a computer-generated voice.

'Molly,' he said, 'Are you awake, luv?'

Molly mumbled something quite incomprehensible. Sounded normal to Arnold.

Molly,' he repeated, 'Molly...'

'Hello, luv,' she said, 'What's the time?'

Arnold looked at the clock on the screen in front of him. It registered 196:06:23. 'Nearly six thirty a.m,' he replied, 'We seem to have been asleep for about six months by my lousy arithmetic.'

'So it all worked! I thought it quite likely that we'd never wake up,' Molly replied.

'Not really, luv, surely. We're far too young to be ready to accept dying as easily as that.'

'No, I suppose not, but it's all still almost too amazing to believe.'

'I believe it all right. I feel famished. What about some breakfast?' Arnold changed his bed into a seat and looked about him. Many other people were doing the same. Someone caught his eye and gave a thumbs-up. Arnold looked at the cats beside him. They were still asleep in their cigar box and would remain so until after landing on the Red Planet. They looked fine. He turned to Molly and asked, 'Did you dream at all, luv?'

'I don't think so,' she replied. 'No, nor me. Funny that.'

After breakfast, Noel Dusk came on the screen. 'I know it's getting to be tedious, but I can report that absolutely everything that could go wrong, went right! We are all awake and there have been no complaints of aches, pains or sickness in general. I am sure you would all like to join me in thanking our medical team. They did a wonderful job.'

This brought forth genuinely rapturous applause and hopes that their skills would continue to be so bright.

Dusk continued: 'On your screens now is the forward view from our lead vessel. You can see Mars very clearly and it really is red – or, at least, reddish – in colour. You will be able to access this view on demand from now onwards. By contrast, here is the view back from our trailing vessel.'

The screen went totally white and featureless.

'No, that's not a fault but it shows our rear view towards the sun which, on the default settings is so bright that it swamps our camera. I will now progressively apply filters to diminish the perceived brightness of our sun. There was little change at first, but gradually it became possible to see the sun as a bright orb filling, at this magnification, about one fifth of the screen. Further dimming was applied after which, Dusk spoke again. 'If you look at the disc of the sun at about four o'clock as we see the image and about a quarter of the way in, you should be able to discern a small black dot. That is the Earth. Seen in silhouette, of course.' He paused, and then, 'We're a long way from home, everyone.' There was an almost religious silence in the cabin as everyone took in the enormity of what they were seeing.

Arnold spoke quietly to Molly: 'You can read about this sort of thing in novels,' he said, 'but it is far, far more inspiring in the flesh.'

Molly took his hand and said, 'Almost makes you religious.'

Arnold snorted quietly, as she knew he would. It was always fun prodding Arnold on that subject. The ship's captain came on to say that the next few hours would be free time for everyone to chat, to look through the ship's telescopes, or even to take a nap.

'You must be bloody joking!' Arnold said, involuntarily, bringing forth a host of similar epithets from his fellow passengers. He was about to unbuckle his harness when Mita and Pita floated up to Molly to ask after the cats. That was nice, thought Arnold. Several other travellers came up to make the same enquiry and to say that they had had some wonderful dreams about them, especially memories of the feline Lazy Susan, as they referred to that wonderful rotation of all eight cats before the big sleep. Those cats really had moved many people to tears, it seemed.

'They won't be woken up until after we land, you know,' Arnold told everyone. People were most understanding but assured him and Molly that they so looked forward to playing with them after that.

They spent the rest of the morning, by which they meant those indications on the clock before noon, moving around the large cabin, finding several friends and chatting about their feelings at this point in their great adventure. There was lots of repetition, as one might expect, but that only served to cement their friendships and secure their well-being.

The last thing that Noel had announced in his morning pep-talk was that he would detail what was planned for the few days ahead. 'I know you will all have read every last word of the Great Book,' he grinned his boyish, quite charming smile, 'but, just in case, I thought I might take you through our plans up to our putting down on Mars. We will spend the next few days examining our machinery, storage and propulsion equipment to make sure all is well. I have no reason to believe that it is not in tip-top order. Those with no formal duties are encouraged to make a holiday of this time, look outside, chat amongst ourselves for it may be a long time before we feel able to spare the time for such luxuries. If anyone has any health issues, however minor, please report to members of the medical team. In due course, everyone will be warned in good time for us to take our seats and strap in for manoeuvres which will bring all three passenger vessels into Mars orbit. All the maths has been done, we're exactly where we ought to be and our velocities are bang on; so it will happen as planned. The plan also calls for the two cargo vessels following us to skip orbit and to land directly on the surface. We have selected the place, in a wide flattish estuary-like area near the south pole of the planet. Our intention is that those cargo ships should gently skid to a halt close to the cliff walls of the estuary about three hundred metres from one another. We hope that we will find a cave in the cliff within another three hundred metres of those places in which to place our power units as soon as we are able. We shall be able to monitor these landings from orbit. If all goes well, we will leave orbit, one at a time and, with the aid of parachutes, gently land some little way from the cliff but by the side of our cargo rockets. Assuming all goes well, each passenger vessel will, under orders from its captain, prepare for what our countrymen used to call "extravehicular activity or EVA".'

'Noel really likes telling that story,' someone across the aisle from Arnold said.

Dusk continued: 'We just plan to go outside.' 'And that joke!' the neighbour added.

'I'll speak to everyone again just before that. I am absolutely confident that everything will go as planned so please relax and enjoy the next few days as you will.'

And so it was. Molly and Arnold were visited by many people they had come to know from the space station in Texas and several others who had sought them out since.

Informal, small gatherings formed from time to time; sometimes rather serious, at others, characterised by hilarity and mirth. It was undeniable, however, that as the day of orbit approached ever closer, conversations became more brittle and laughter ever more forced. Meanwhile, however, they had enjoyed some more than acceptable meals from Gaston Bloominghell's kitchens back on Earth and there were many bets laid on what they contained.

Well, push came to shove, and the ship's captain ordered everyone to strap into his or her seat, to put on headphones and prepare for the engines to fire. The first manoeuvre would be to use small thrusters to turn the vessel almost right round so that when the main thrusters fired the ship would begin to slow down. Not turning exactly about meant that the vessels would not collide with one another and would begin separate approaches to different but closely similar orbit locations. Passengers would be able to watch proceedings on their screens and to select different camera orientations at will, as before. There would be three main firings with small course corrections between each.

The captain came on speaker after each manoeuvre to confirm that all was hunky-dory and that they should relax and enjoy the view of Mars coming up beneath them. When all firings had finished including some minute last minute corrections, the three passenger vehicles were coasting along within a hundred metres of one another, each a few metres further from the Martian surface than the next in line. Their courses were stable and, had they wanted, they could have remained in these positions, probably for an eternity. The captain took control of their camera angles so that everyone could see what was to happen next. And that was to watch the approach of the cargo vessels. Some twenty minutes later, they came into view on a trajectory below them, pointing backwards and heading slowly to the surface. When they seemed almost at the surface, but that was difficult to gauge from above, each vessel in turn deployed four enormous parachutes but were lost from view because the orbiting passenger ships had moved on. By the time the latter had completed another circuit of Mars, the cargo vessels were close together on the ground and near the cliff edge of a wide "riverbed" – although such measures were relative from our position, Arnold thought.

The captain came on the blower again. 'That's the first bit done, folks, exactly to plan. Now it's our turn. Hold tight!' Almost immediately, the thrusters began to fire and, ever so gradually, the ship began to approach the surface.

Molly reached out to grasp Arnold's hand. 'Oh, my love,' she cried out and he gripped her hand tightly. As he did so, the ship began to shudder. A number of passengers called out at that point. The captain came on the speaker: 'It's all right, everyone! That's our parachutes deploying. It will all get calm very soon!' and so it did as, under rocket and parachute power, they glided down to the surface, landing as planned on their side. All noise had ceased, and they came to a complete standstill. They were, however, upside down.

'Captain again! All's well but do not unfasten your seat belts or you might fall out onto your heads! Don't worry but there will be some funny noises from outside as we extend some arms which are designed to roll us over. I repeat: everything is absolutely fine. Ladies and gentlemen: welcome to Mars!' His words were greeted with a wave of laughter and applause as relief set in.

Arnold, ever the realist, turned to Molly and said quietly, 'We're on Mars, luv. For good.' He took her hand and leaned over to kiss her. It was not to be the last time they had tears in their eyes.

10

After three days on Martian soil – or should we say regolith, Arnold wondered for he had looked up that word on Giggle – during which everyone had had a chance to go outside through secure airlocks in their spacesuits and walk as far as the other passenger vessels; to experience the low gravity of Mars, which being a little over one third of that on Earth allowed them to hop up to three to five feet off the ground depending on how hard they tried in their cumbersome suits; and to look at the sun through their protective visors, a sun which was far more orange than what they were used to on Earth and much smaller too.

After three days, Wesley and Jenny Wright suggested that it was time to wake the cats up again. This, thought Arnold, was going to be an important moment for now they would see how their darling pussycats would take to a new life, not as circus show-offs in zero gravity, but as proper little people. The appropriate litter facilities had been set up once more and, of course, it was not anticipated that they would venture outside, for no suitable spacesuits had been constructed for them. They would otherwise have as free an access to all parts of number two passenger pod as the patience and generosity of its human inhabitants would allow. It had been made crystal clear to everyone that, should any member of the expedition seek respite from the attentions of these moving furballs, they should contact Molly or Arnold who would immediately remove them. The cats, that is.

It might have been fun to record how a gang of eight miaowing feline soldiers set forth to conquer their space pod. So it might, but that didn't happen. The cats all woke up completely, just as they had before and just as their human friends had nearly two weeks earlier, but they were ever so clingy. They loved their mummy, and they loved their daddy, and they were going nowhere. Arnold and Molly adored every moment, every twirl of a tail around their arms and around their legs, every wipe of fur across their faces. The purring was deafening. Those cats didn't need the power of human speech. They made their feelings abundantly clear. Jenny and Wesley left them all to it in the certainty that their part in this whole business was well done.

For the sake of completeness and accurate reporting, it should be admitted that this whole nauseating love-in lasted for a good hour and that further description would serve no real purpose. For us, that is.

Eventually, it occurred to the cats that they might be hungry, and they made their feelings plain. Arnold led them like the pied piper to an area which had been allocated for cat-feeding long ago. There was a large cupboard set aside there containing all sorts of cat goodies and from which Arnold opened a couple of packets of both hard and soft foods, hoping that there would always be a sufficient supply. There were several bowls in the cupboard too, so that before long, there took place the familiar feeding frenzy – no, it wasn't a frenzy: ravenous was a better word, he thought – he recalled from so long ago. Neither he nor Molly had dreamed during their hibernation, so neither, he assumed, had the cats. Accordingly, although normal feeding actually was a very long time ago, it shouldn't appear that way. Theory is a wonderful thing, Arnold Forbutt. Well, the cats cleared their bowls, and each one seemed satisfied, judging by the licking of chops and wiping of their faces by their paws, by the stretching and arching of their bodies. Adjacent to the cats' food cupboard, someone had very thoughtfully provided several small cubby holes lined with soft, foamy material. It took little time for the cats to recognise these places for what they undoubtedly were, and to climb into them, in ones, twos and as a threesome, to curl up and sleep off their breakfast. How on earth can they go back to sleep after more than six month's hibernation? Arnold marvelled. Surely, Arnold, you know better than that.

Even Arnold would have acknowledged that there were bigger fish to fry at that time. Not in Arnold's department, of course but, for the sake of completeness and reportage, it is only right to spend a little time, at least, describing the big picture (BigPicture). One of the first things planned after landing and safety checks was to set up the power supplies to run their accommodation and construction facilities. A powerful, though modestly small, nuclear-powered electricity generator had been included on board each supply vessel. There was one in each, not so much to make sure of adequate power supply but in case one of the supply vessels had been lost. Indeed, there was a fair degree of duplication of all kinds of supplies between the big rockets for just that reason. Nevertheless, the supply modules had landed, as planned so wonderfully, close to the edge of a dry river basin. That edge took the form of a significantly high and rocky cliff: some thirty metres or more high. A small party of engineers went in search of any cave-like formation within that cliff for it had been hoped to put the nuclear power units inside such caves, partly for protection from sandstorms which were well-known to blow across much of the planet, although they had planned to land on this particular side of the dry estuary – for that seemed a good description of the low, flat and wide basin they found themselves in – because the prevailing winds on Mars in that general location were known to blow away from that cliff. On the far side of the estuary, as they would confirm in the weeks to come, a considerable depth of sand had built up against the cliff margin, but their side was almost completely free of it. They also intended to take advantage of the rock in the cliff as a secondary layer of insulation from any slight radiation leakage which was inevitable in view of the limited amount of lead shielding they had been able to lift off from the Earth. The power units were completely self-contained and sealed, although access for repairs was possible under duress. Each unit had enough radioactive nuclear fuel to keep power generation going for about fifty years, during which time it was hoped that further deliveries of fuel could be made from Mother Earth.

Luck was certainly with them, for the expeditionary team soon found several good-sized nooks and crannies in the cliff, well-concealed behind rock walls which appeared to be very dense, hard-wearing and likely to be pretty well opaque to radiation. They downloaded a small fork-lift truck from each of the supply ships and began to shift the power supplies to their secure homes for the decades to come, and of course, to check their integrity so far as radiation leakage was concerned. It all went very smoothly, and within five days, they had set up a power nexus some thirty metres from the cliffs and the power sources they now housed. From that point on, all that was necessary for powering up their machinery and accommodation on a permanent basis was to plug into that central power board. The plugs were heavy duty features, of course, but the principle was simple enough.

Work then began on conversion of the supply rocket bodies, one at a time, into large living units affording far more space and comfort than they had enjoyed for the last seven months. That required the construction of several storage units for the supplies and equipment carried within those rockets, food stores, and of workshops within which metal-forming equipment and the like could be housed in safety. The workshops would be equipped with airlocks so that operations could be carried out without the need to wear spacesuits. All these supplementary units had been transported in disassembled manner, rather like the flatpacks beloved (or not) of homebuilders. It was inevitable that some wag had muttered something about including the correct-sized Allen key and instructions with words. Of course, the workshops had to be made completely airtight and, although appropriate seals were built into the sections, their assembly had to be conducted with all due care. It had been hoped to accomplish these "outhouse" constructions within two weeks. They were finished in thirteen days. Dusk was beaming all over the place. It took slightly less than one more week to transfer all contents of the first supply vessel into the storage sheds. For the sake of clarity and completeness, one must observe that one of the storage units was a bloody big shed. Also, for the sake of completeness and transparency, it is to be noted that the first accident of the expeditionary force occurred at this time. It happened as a door to the storage unit slipped from a forklift onto the hard ground below. Of course, with Martian gravity being much less than Earth's gravity, the door hit the ground with far less force than was familiar. Conversely, however, the door had been made far flimsier than it might have been on Earth for there were no known marauders to damage it. Furthermore, it was a simple door, as there was no need for it to be airtight: there was no airlock on the storage unit like that on the workshop door. The bottom line was that the fall warped the door a little so that it didn't quite close at the bottom corner away from the hinge. There was a degree of embarrassment by the forklift driver, but nobody was unduly bothered by the accident. Anyway, much later, other similar buildings were to be erected when it became time to convert the second supply ship into accommodation.

There followed several more weeks of work in the machine shop, followed by transference of parts back into the large rocket body, which had been thoroughly cleaned of any residue from the fuel it had contained, and subsequent conversion of the large space inside into many rooms with many purposes – all, of course, having been planned in meticulous detail years earlier.

Jenny Wright was the source of a surprising piece of news for the Forbutts one day. There was another group of – in this case four – cats belonging to someone in passenger vessel number three. Neither Molly nor Arnold had heard a word about them before that moment. That was hardly surprising, for a certain Mel and Trish McConnel had smuggled their pets into the party without anyone knowing.

'How did they survive the hibernation?' Arnold had asked immediately. Apparently, Mel and Trish had each pushed a couple of cats down into their spacesuits, rather like the professional cigar cases which had been supplied to the Forbutts for their cats and thus held fast. Their cats had been given knock-out pills ground into a little milk, and at the same time their carers had taken theirs. How they had survived so careless a procedure is anyone's guess. But they had, and were all well and amusing themselves and others in that passenger pod.

Jenny asked if it would be all right with Arnold and Molly to take these four cats on board for a sort of "sleep-over" for the night. Naturally, they were only too happy to oblige. Would their brood be so accommodating, however? They needn't have worried. All twelve cats got on like a house on fire and it was agreed that sometime later there might be a "return match" over in the other passenger pod. It came as no surprise to anyone, except to Arnold that is, when Jenny announced, several months later, that two of Mel and Trish's white cats were pregnant. 'In kitten,' she said.

'How on earth did that happen, Mother?' asked Arnold. 'The usual way, luv,' she replied.

'Yes, but they were only together for a couple of nights,' Arnold protested. 'Didn't you see the engagement ring then, luv?' Molly said with a slightly pitying look on her face.

Arnold had run out of things to say. However, even Molly was surprised when, some eight weeks later, word came that Mel and Trish's cats had given birth to ten tiny kittens, most of which were white with black streaks but with a couple being pure black.

'Personage was busy!' Arnold mused.

Naturally, special arrangements had to be made to raise and house all these kittens for there was absolutely no suggestion that they be culled. There was, however, a degree of carelessness in how it was done over in passenger vessel three and those kittens got all over the place as soon as they were able to stagger around. And then walk. And run. And climb. Oh! The delightful little darlings. More people in that pod than you might have expected fell completely in love with these running, jumping bundles of joy. They engendered so much love in the place that two things happened in consequence.

The first was that May Wheatley, wife of the dashing young electrical engineer, Peter Wheatley, fell pregnant.

For the sake of probity and completeness, let there be no suggestion of any abnormal, bestial indiscretion in this news; rather that one event inspired, rather than engendered, another.

And the second consequence was that two of the young kittens somehow escaped through the airlock into the low-pressure, low-oxygen Martian atmosphere outside. It probably occurred while unsuspecting, unobservant, people were moving through the seal in their spacesuits. There was a considerable degree of upset when this was discovered, as you might expect, but a search for the poor things' dead bodies outside the passenger pod proved fruitless. At first, it had been supposed that the corpses had been inadvertently kicked away somewhere, but surely still close to the airlock. A very thorough search yielded nothing. Poor little Clarence and Unity – for those were the poor mites' names – had vanished. Many people resident on all three passenger pods were more than a little upset by this news. Arnold was especially saddened by the news.

'Oh, Molly, that's not good,' he said quietly to her, 'I'd be devastated if anything like that should happen to our lot.

Come to think about it, they are our lot in a way. Sort of grandchildren, I suppose.'

After about three months, construction in what had been support vessel number one, was complete and Noel Dusk held a party in there for everyone. That is, for some nine hundred people. That's a large number of people to house in one tin tube. It gives one a good idea of the size of that place. The rocket body had been divided into many compartments, some large and some small: one, in which the party was being held, being extremely large. Dusk explained that this assembly hall was intended for large collective gatherings of all kinds: a party as this one today, a concert hall maybe; for any gathering which people might feel a need. It was important, he said, that there be spaces which would allow for all kinds of activity so that some degree of "normality" might be enjoyed in their new home. Elsewhere within the vessel, the Martians would find private accommodations of various sizes, according to need and/or desire and yet further on, there were two separate gymnasiums, and three restaurants.

'You will also notice that several windows have been inserted in the structure so that we may have many views of our red environment and that we may begin to learn that this is really our home. This is not intended to be a place of incessant work – even though there is still much to do in the preliminary phase – but a place to live, to think, and to learn to love.' Noel really was becoming something of a poet. Alcohol was served that day.

In the months that followed, similar conversion of the body of the second support ship was accomplished and a bridging tunnel between the two had been constructed. Shortly after that time, everyone had taken up residence in one or other of the large pods which had been named Refuge1 and Refuge2. People moved freely about these spaces, respecting those parts which had been claimed as private, of course. Some people's quarters were larger than others, though not by too much. This caused no problems of jealousy or entitlement, for some folk preferred to be cosier than others. The assignment of quarters had all gone very smoothly and everyone was happy with his or her lot. The cats, of course, were more than content, having free run of the whole place.

Although there was still work to be done in gutting and refurbishing the three original passenger pods, work slowed a little to allow for an increase in free time and for reconnaissance of the countryside around and beyond their camp. It was during one such exploration that one of the environmental scientists discovered that bordering the cliff bottom were channels in the regolith which seemed quite deep and to run for miles. It was confirmation that the ground on which they were camped was the bottom of an ancient wide river or estuary and that those small, deep gullies at the base of the bordering cliff had been cut by once-running water. Maybe there was still water down there, or ice at any rate? The geologists began to plan their explorations, for water or ice would be a great find. Meanwhile other members of the geological and chemistry teams had already set about examining the regolith in the valley as a possible source of rocket fuel and other important materials. Yet a third team were doing something similar up on the clifftop. They had brought all manner of analytical equipment with them: mass spectrometry, radiology, general chemical analysis and lots of words of which Arnold had never before heard. They glowed with confidence and quiet excitement. That was something which Arnold could recognise, and it gave confidence.

And, talking about confidence, May Wheatley was about to pop. Her pregnancy had gone so smoothly that Peter had begun to wonder if Noel Dusk had had a hand in organising it all. They had decided to take the surprise. May specifically asked that the sex of her child not be revealed to her; they did, however, know from ultrasound examinations, that she was not expecting a multiple birth. Things were going so well that it would be fair to say that their biggest problem was to decide on a name for their baby. Many suggestions were offered by their friends, names like Marti, Martin or Marsha and they happily took all suggestions on board. When the time came, Jenny Wright was in attendance and had to suffer numerous comments along the lines of 'Don't get confused with the cats, Jenny!' and so on. With Peter by her side and some nine hundred fellow passengers rooting for her just a baby-cry away, May safely gave birth to her first child after no more than one hour's labour. It was a boy, and it had a good pair of lungs. The cry was heard outside the birthing suite and the whole place immediately went wild with joy, shouts of congratulations and messaging going back and forth all over the settlement. The Wheatleys had long ago taken to Arnold and Molly's occasional use of a Yorkshire accent so when they asked the Forbutts to view the babe, it was appropriate for them to announce that having taken advice from so many well-wishers, they had decided to adopt Arnold Forbutt's suggestion as a name for their son. FustOne Wheatley was, thus, the first true Martian. Molly and Arnold were invited to be honorary grandparents. Never having been parents themselves, they were more than a little apprehensive about what that might mean down the line.

'Don't worry,' Mel said, 'just think of him as one of your lovely cats and it will all fall into place.' She should know, having been Mother to three, now grown-up, children as well as to innumerable cats.

A bit of a knees-up was held in honour of the Wheatley family in general and of FustOne, in particular. Noel came to beam upon the family and alcohol was served. The arrival of the first Martian had a deep impact on many people's thoughts as its significance slowly trickled deep down into their subconscious.

11

They had been on the Red Planet now for well over a year: Earth year, that is. They had experienced two dust storms, one of them being really severe which had continued unabated for nearly two weeks, but it did no damage to their home or, indeed to any of their facilities for, as anticipated long ago, the wind had blown over their heads. Their buildings were more or less in the lee of the storm. There had been many exploratory walks and rides – for they had brought electric quad bikes with them for that purpose – both on what they commonly referred to as the riverbed, as well as along the cliff top. The geologists had found a number of very useful minerals, but Arnold had no idea what they were, only that they had produced quite some measure of excitement. The biggest – or better – the most important, discovery had been of water-ice deep down in some of those gullies they had spotted early on. That had been identified by lowering miniature cameras down into some of those gullies some way from their encampment. There was even a suggestion in one place down there of an underground cave system, obviously having been formed by water erosion long ago, and it was hoped to pursue this further in search of liquid water, should the subsoil be warmer than the air-cooled regolith above, as could be expected. Some quite feverish activity had been under way in this regard for some weeks now.

Everyone's spirits were far higher than had been feared before they blasted off from Earth so long ago. Yes, it was only a year or so, but it seemed far longer. They were Martians now, and proud of it. There were, naturally, moments of quiet and sorrow when one remembered someone or something back on Earth (not back home, however. It was not thought of in that way anymore), but these passed. There was always so much to do: the work in developing their new home; entertainment, much imported from Earth, of course, but also an increasing, if still small amount of home-grown entertainment in the form of group singing, bridge clubs and the like, sports, book clubs and, to the surprise of some, dining out. The food available in the eating houses varied from more of Gaston Bloominghell's geometric, but tasty, shapes to inventions made from crops grown in the local hydroponic sections carved out of one of the old passenger pods. The hydroponics had begun from the moment of lift-off from Earth but had, as planned, become successful enough to occupy the whole of one of the old passenger pods these days. Many bemoaned the lack of meat but there were several quite acceptable substitutes. Certainly, from a purely medical point of view, they were plentifully supplied with all important vitamins and textures to provide necessary roughage. The taste was different rather than worse. A still had been set up but produced only enough alcohol to satisfy people for special occasions. Folk had become used to a minimal alcohol diet and, of course, those miserable medics were only too delighted. It also meant that there was less chance of unnecessary confrontations. It wasn't so much that life was prissy on Mars, more that it was careful. And that was essential.

By the time the second year came around, explorations in a region some two hundred kilometres from base were being conducted. By now, water had been found underground – and less deep than had been feared because of peculiarities of the underground rock formations which funnelled warmth from very deep down to regions which were not too remote from the surface. There was plenty and it didn't need too much work to be made potable. More to the point, however, is that it provided raw material for hydrogen as a fuel and oxygen for breathing amongst other uses, all by electrolysis powered by their nuclear power centres.

Talking about those nuclear power plants, it had been discovered that there had been a slight breach in the radiation shield of one of them. There was no great danger to the settlers because the plants were placed well back into the caves which had been selected for that very purpose in the first week of the colony and so there were considerable thicknesses of rock between the radioactive sources and the outside world. Nevertheless, it had been a worry and had taken quite some time to repair, for engineers could only work close to an imperfectly protected radio-active source for so many minutes a day.

But the repair had been accomplished, and all had been well again for some months by this time.

There was one other problem. Somehow, some of the food-stores were rather smaller than they should be. It was obviously a problem of accounting, but the losses had not yet been rationalised. There was plenty of food in store, however, so the matter had not garnered any high degree of urgency. It had been noted and was "under examination".

Meanwhile, Dusk's businesses back on Earth were going from strength to strength so there was plenty of cash in the pot for more rocket launches to Mars. It was apparent that such was Dusk's whole business motivation, and two complete service rockets were due in two months' time. There was also talk of some further passenger ships in two- or three-years' time. Noel's great ambition (GreatAmbition) to be the founder of man's colonisation of a second planet was firming up by the year.

It was around this time that Molly and Arnold joined a small expeditionary group to explore some of the territory along the cliff edge in the opposite direction from where all previous explorations had taken place. They regarded the whole thing as a day or so out, a sort of holiday. They were well-provisioned with food, drink and cameras. They went as part of a group of twelve. Everyone wore spacesuits, of course, because of the low air pressure and poor oxygen levels outside. They could barely hear one another through soundwaves in that thin air but conversed readily enough via wifi and Bluetooth links, spacesuit to spacesuit. They were all being carried in one of the special personnel carriers which Musk's team had designed and built back on Earth. It was capable of traversing quite uneven ground and had been a roaring success. It was powered by some of Dusk's batteries which were charged by the radioactive sources back at their Martian home. They had decided to travel continuously for four hours before stopping to picnic and make plans for exploration. Apart from that bit of planning, they had planned nothing except to stay close to the cliff. It was quite adventurous of them, really.

They were quite peckish by the time they stopped, so that food took top priority in everyone's minds. By this time on Mars, their cooking section had prepared a fair array of tasty dishes and, although Gaston Bloominghell had made some long-distance contributions which were generally much appreciated, they also had many more familiar, or at least familiar-looking, dishes available. They had brought a fair selection with them. Arnold and Molly even had some fair imitations of faggots with them. They offered them around but had no takers.

'More for us, luv,' Arnold whispered, with a twinkle in his eye.

Those preferring grits took a similar line, so honours were, more or less, even. Alcohol was not carried on the trip. One of Dusk's rules, readily agreed to by just about everybody, was that booze could only be consumed back at base. Although the Martians had grown a little blasé over the years, the dangers of being in the Martian environment were never to be forgotten.

They had worn their spacesuits on the journey out of an overabundance of caution for their vehicle was pressurised and filled with a breathable atmosphere. However, there was always the possibility of some leakage in their cabin owing to excessive vibrations as they covered unknown terrain, so suits were worn. Once they had stopped, they were free to remove their helmets and eat normally.

Otherwise, they would have had to rely on liquids and tubes and all that sort of thing. Arnold was not the only one present to dislike such restrictions.

After everyone had had their fill, they donned their helmets once more, the airlock in the cabin was cracked and they all filed out onto "martiofirma", as Arnold was wont to discuss Martian ground. They split up into three groups of four and set about a bit of exploring. Very soon, the lead group, which included Molly and Arnold, began following the runnels near to the cliff face. Those runnels had been a nearly continuous feature for the whole of their journey and, meanwhile, the cliffs had probably doubled in height compared with their size back at base. A sizeable boulder blocked their progress at this point, but it was easy to walk around. As they did so, they found that those runnels quite suddenly widened out into three crevasses down which one could easily fall. They drew the attention of the other two groups to their discovery and suggested that ladders, ropes and similar gear, which their vehicle carried on its roof-rack, should be brought forward. This was done and two of the fitter members of the group began to descend into one of the crevasses. It turned out that the three separate crevasses visible from the surface were all interconnected immediately below ground. After a bit more searching, they even found an easier way down there, one that comprised a quite gentle slope from the surface to some ten metres or so from the surface. Furthermore, the ground under foot was clear of loose pebbles and the path down was sufficiently uneven to provide good footholds. In short, Molly and Arnold were easily able to walk down into the underground space. Their companions offered their hands and arms in support, but they weren't necessary.

It was, of course, dark down there, so the next step was for someone to go back to their vehicle to fetch lights. They found enough space to stand comfortably and survey their surroundings. They were in a moderately large cave and it was as clear as day that it had been formed by erosion, presumably by water, over many years – presumably centuries. Arnold remembered going into the Stump Cross Caverns near Grassington, north of Leeds in Yorkshire, and this was a poor imitation of those. They began to explore the extremities of the cave when one of their number suddenly called out that he had found a sizeable hole in the bottom of the cave near to one end. It was easily large enough for them to climb down and explore further. Before doing so, however, they took pains to document everything they had found so far and to transmit images of it all back to base. After all, should bad fortune befall them, those who followed must be kept properly informed. Molly thought it all frightfully exciting and was enjoying herself immensely. Mike Brawton, or "Braveheart" as he was being called as leader of their expedition, then began to descend into the hole. He was tethered to a slender rope held by Mel Crouder but he needn't have worried overmuch. The rope was slender and, on Earth, would have been described as lightweight. Low Martian gravity meant that such tethers needed not to be as strong as those back on Earth. The hole into which he had descended wasn't vertical but rather took the form of a roughly cylindrical passage, or tube, leading downwards at an angle which would have been considered steep on Earth, but under the much- reduced Martian gravity, Mike's descent seemed simple and safe enough. He had descended some four metres when the tube changed direction by nearly ninety degrees. Mike commented that the way forward, however, was just as easy. His tethering rope was, fortunately, long enough for him to continue for some distance yet. Something like twenty-five metres had to be paid out before Mike stopped dead in his tracks, calling back with great excitement.

'My God! You must come and see this,' he yelled, and continued, 'It's all perfectly safe. It's probably best if everyone is tied for safety's sake, but I doubt if that's really essential. Bring plenty of light with you, and it might be a good idea to leave at least one rope tethered to your position in case we have need of it on the return.'

Arnold and Molly, fit youngsters of just 82 and 73, hurried to follow Mike down the tube. Their colleagues were full of admiration for their pluck and fitness. Life on Mars really had improved their physique in some mysterious fashion. Arnold led the way in case Molly slipped. He needn't have worried. They both made it down to join Mike in less than five minutes even though they were being very careful. Mike was standing on a reasonably flat area which was easily large enough for twenty people to gather. He had set a floodlight on wide angle so as to illuminate a wide area. As soon as Molly and Arnold had joined Mike, they were able to view their surroundings. It was utterly amazing, breath-taking, awe-inspiring. They found themselves in an enormous cave, perhaps a hundred metres long by sixty wide, although it was difficult to describe it in those terms for the shape of the cave was very complex and, at first glance, it was not at all clear how many possible exits there were all over the place. And, like those Stump Cross Caverns, stalactites and stalagmites were in abundance. They were mostly red, like the surface of Mars outside, but there were many striations in colour. It was, by the way, incredibly beautiful.

While Molly and Arnold stood, turned and gawped at everything around them, the rest of the picnic party made their way down the tube.

'I wonder if Alice will pop up soon?' Arnold joked.

For the sake of security and best practise, Mel contacted base to inform them of their findings. With exemplary foresight, Mel had left a simple communications relay device up in the first, small cave, for just this eventuality. Radio and visual contact with base were well-nigh perfect and the holiday party heard appreciative noises and envy from those back home.

After bringing yet more ropes down from their touring vehicle, together with crampons and all such climbing gear, the party agreed to split up into six pairs for what would most certainly be the first of many explorations of these caves. The ground under foot was quite dry and not at all crumbly, so it was simple even for Arnold and Molly to play their part. They simply followed their noses, although they snook glances at their colleagues' progress and tried to keep well away from them, the idea being that they might, as a group, cover as wide an area as possible. When they had gone about a hundred metres from their starting point and some twenty metres further down, they stopped and turned back to look at where they had come from. A red light had been left there as a beacon for the return trip. Now the cavern could be viewed in all its glory. It was, indeed, literally truly cavernous. Arnold observed to Molly, more than a little seriously, that the place would make a wonderful home.

'Provided that one didn't mind being away from the open skies, living like rabbits down a hole, the place would make a superb, cathedral-like space. Of course, there would be the problem of making it airtight so that one could move around without these damn spacesuits.'

'I think it will be a while before Noel takes this on,' Molly, ever practical, replied.

They were standing on a reasonably flat area of ground, a sort of ledge, but a way forward was not yet clear to them. The route had seemed obvious from their previous position but when push came to shove, it seemed that they had hit a dead end. Arnold moved to the end of the ledge, looking for any way forward that they had missed. Molly went on about it being obvious that they had come to a dead end and that there was nothing for it but to turn back, but Arnold, being Arnold, simply had to try. He found nothing helpful. He knocked on the cave wall at various points to see if anything sounded hollow. It didn't. He stamped his foot on the ground for the same reason and struck luckier than he could have wished for. A sizeable hole opened up underneath him, something like a metre square. Gravity, having the same properties on Mars as on Earth, acted in the only way it knew. Arnold disappeared from view down the plughole before Molly could even cry out. Very gingerly, Molly approached the edge of the hole and shone her torch down. Arnold had fallen some twenty metres before coming to rest on a large and uneven area of what may, or may not, have been the cave bottom. His tether was fortunately long enough so that a good length still remained up near Molly.

'Arnold, darling, are you alright?' she called. Is this how we are to die, she thought? Down a rabbit hole on the Red Planet? The ignominy of it!

No, this was not the way it was to be. Arnold called back to her... but I must digress at this point for the sake of clarity and good reportage and say that Arnold's and Molly's exchanges were via their electronic, Bluetooth whatsit, rather than by calling through the air as if in Arnold's favourite Stump Cross Caves back in Yorkshire... Arnold called back that he was all right. A little shaken but the relatively low Martian gravity had been kind to him. He thought that his spacesuit was undamaged. But when he tried to get to his feet, he let out a loud cry of agony and sat straight back down again.

'I think I've twisted my ankle or something,' he told Molly. 'I'll try again in a minute...' However, Molly's reception of Arnold's words had broken up very badly. She told Arnold, who twisted himself into a sitting position but apparently said nothing. After some moments, Molly repeated her message. She heard some crackling sound but no more. Molly, who wasn't particularly savvy when it came to technical matters, had nevertheless, picked up a bit from the communications training they had received back on Earth in Texas. She switched her communications from Bluetooth to WiFi mode and tried again. Once more, all she got from Arnold was crackling. She turned her device to general calling and reported Arnold's accident. Mike replied, saying that the party would get to her as soon as possible, but meanwhile she was to do nothing. He was especially concerned lest Arnold's spacesuit had suffered damage, especially any leakage to the outside vanishingly low-pressure Martian atmosphere. Mita and Pita, who were in the party, called Molly with reassuring noises obviously aimed at calming her down. That was very sweet of them, but they had misjudged Molly who, though naturally concerned about Arnold's predicament, was no weeper; no little wifey. At least that's what Molly thought about herself.

Meanwhile, down below, Arnold was trying to come to terms with his predicament. He had deduced that, while he could hear everything Molly said, she couldn't hear him. So he must have damaged his backpack in the fall. He knew that Molly would report back to the rest of the party. There was little he could do but look around him while he waited for help to arrive. He soon focussed on two things. One was that the colour of the rocks and stalagmites and such around him were different. Instead of varying shades of red, they were strongly striated in yellows, greens and even blues. And, when he touched these structures, he noticed immediately that they were slippery. He moved his gloved hand back and forth and concluded that everything around him was wet, perhaps slimy. He remembered that one of Dusk's expeditionary parties had found water not too long after they had landed on this planet, but that discovery had been many, many kilometres away and only via a miniature camera on the end of a rope. Was the water here connected with that? He couldn't see any running water, but the fact that the ground on which he sat was wet surely meant that running water could not be far away. Furthermore, the fact that the ground around him was wet rather than slippery with ice, meant that the temperature in that part of the cave must be higher than zero degrees centigrade. Outside the caves, on the planet's surface, the temperature was incredibly cold. The spacesuit back-pack contained all sorts of technical gubbins to keep its wearer warm. Arnold felt comfortable in his suit and presumed that all that technology was working well. Where did all the heat come from to melt ice down there? No doubt the geologists in the colony would look into that pretty soon.

Arnold moved rather little for he found it too painful to try harder just then. He also noted that he had now lost reception from other members of the party as well as from Molly. He wasn't particularly concerned about that, for everyone knew where he was, and help was on its way. So there he was, sitting in silence, taking in some quite breathtaking scenery. Arnold was quite content to wait. The silence was quite wonderful. Such a change, Arnold thought, not to have the perpetual babble of chatter on the airways, back and forth. Human conversation was wonderful, of course, but occasionally, so was the lack of it. Arnold concentrated as he listened to the silence. After some time, he became aware that there wasn't perfect silence. Some low frequencies were penetrating his spacesuit from outside. He assumed they were just the remnants of echoes from his colleagues moving around elsewhere in the huge cave. It had to be that, didn't it? Reflections of sound, making echoes within the cathedral. One thing about the sound which Arnold noticed particularly was its soothing character. He could have listened to that calming bath of sound forever.

Well, it turned out that he couldn't, because Mike, the leader of the picnic party, as Arnold had described their outing to Molly some hours earlier, suddenly appeared, hanging from a rope immediately above him. He was indicating to Arnold to move to one side so that he might complete his descent. Arnold tried standing once more, but his ankle would have none of it. Instead, he shuffled sideways on his bottom. The low gravity made this much easier than he had expected. Mike completed his descent and placed his helmet against Arnold's. 'Can you hear me, Arnold? How are you?' he enquired. The sound of his voice through the helmets was perfectly clear.

'I think I've sprained my ankle. Or broken it. But I think it's just a sprain. I can't stand though. Otherwise, I'm okay, thanks.'

Mike tied a couple of spare ropes, which he had brought down with him, around Arnold and when he was satisfied with his knots or whatever, called up to other members of the party to begin hauling the wounded soldier back up. Arnold could hear what Mike was saying, even when their helmets weren't touching. It seemed there was enough of an atmosphere outside to conduct the sound of speech.

Well, the rescue went well. In due course, Arnold had been hauled back to the Martian surface and into the expeditionary vehicle. Arnold complained strongly about feeling cold during the ascent back to the surface, which Mike put down to damage to the backpack temperature control system. Mike insisted that everybody return to the vehicle and that the party go back to base. They had all the time in the world to return to these caves with more equipment so that specialists could go over the place with a fine toothcomb. Mike was still concerned about Arnold's spacesuit, but that assumed low importance now that they were all back in their bus with its proper, breathable atmosphere and everyone had removed his helmet. Arnold was apologising to all and sundry about bringing their expedition to a premature close and all and sundry told him not to be silly and that he hadn't caused the ground under him to collapse.

'These things happen, Arnold,' they said.

Molly, that strong non-wifey partner and wife, finally burst into tears with relief at not losing her beloved husband. Before leaving the caves, Mike left a marker and radio beacon there to help follow-up expeditions, and then suggested that they all have a bite to eat. Arnold began his meal with a few painkillers and soon felt quite well again. On arrival back at base, Arnold's spacesuit was removed ready for examination by the technocrats. Arnold was not the only one to notice that, not only did his gloves and spacesuit bottom feel slimy with some green/blue substance which looked for all the world like lichen and moss, but also smelt strongly and rather odd at first. Until, that is, Arnold suddenly announced that the smell reminded him strongly of catnip. He was unaware of any mosses or lichen back on Earth which smelt of catnip but maybe here things were different? His spacesuit was to be studied by the biochemists and botanists. Wesley Wright examined Arnold most carefully and declared that he had suffered nothing worse than an ankle sprain. He had been very lucky.

Later that night, in bed with Molly, Arnold told of the sound he had enjoyed while he was waiting to be rescued. 'I've been thinking, Molly,' he said, 'About that sound. I can't tell the others. They'd only laugh, but I could swear it sounded just like hundreds of cats purring. It was lovely. You'd have loved the sound, luv.'

Molly was quite taken with Arnold's description. 'What a lovely thought,' she said.

12

And so it happened. Tedious to record every nut and bolt, every gain and every loss. Suffice to say, that the colony grew its success and increased its number. By year twelve, there were four thousand Martians, all housed, well-fed and entertained. All as proud as punch of their achievement.

All the original cats were still around, much to Molly and Arnold's surprise. Blondie had given birth to a litter of five kittens, with colours ranging from brown to pale ginger. They had been given names only as their personalities had emerged, names which were even more confusing than those sired by Personage much earlier. Maybe an age of fourteen for Snowflake et al. was not so great but the point here is that they frolicked about as if they were youngsters of two or three. For that matter, Arnold himself was now in his early nineties, and Molly had made it into her eighties a couple of years earlier, and yet they felt much younger.

They had few medical issues, certainly fewer than when they had left Earth and, no doubt because of continuing exercise, encouraged and supervised by Jenny and Wesley Wright, their muscle tone had improved rather than deteriorated. There was no doubt that Martian life was good for them. Something was definitely helping to keep them young, but such things are so hard to identify or demonstrate without inviting derision. There was no question, however, of what Arnold referred to a Benjamin Button effect, of course, for this was real life, not some kind of imaginative novelist's fiction.

Recently, a rather odd report had been sent from the remains of the mirror group back on Mother Earth. It was in the form of an enquiry.

'Were the Martians (they had, at last been accorded that title back on Earth) aware of water-ice along the margins of the wadi or riverbed around the area of their habitation?'

Apparently, people looking through high-power telescopes at Mars from afar had begun to notice white and silver steaks near the cliffs where they lived. The Martians looked about their settlement but saw nothing. It was a puzzle. But then someone pointed out that those who had seen the phenomenon from Earth had done so through "integrating" telescopy, meaning that their images had been collected over time – often for the period of a Martian day or so – and added together to produce what the layman might call a time-composite. They had forwarded their images and it was undeniable that streaks of silver abounded in the vicinity of the encampment and, indeed, for miles around. It was a great puzzle (GreatPuzzle).

People took to looking out of their windows to see if they could catch a view of this phenomenon but were completely unsuccessful. Arnold pointed out that the windows were set too high to afford a view close to their accommodation and, in particular one of the ground near the little ravines adjacent to the cliff.

Accordingly, he set up a continuous view through the external cameras and put it on continuous record. When he began to study the playback next day, he was annoyed to find an unsteadiness in the video record, for he observed many streaks form across the frame, streaks of silver and grey. He then had the bright idea of slowing the play-back down by a factor of ten. His eyes popped out of his head. Those streaks were nothing less than silver, grey and white cats streaking across the field of view. Dozens of them. Perhaps hundreds. Many of them had dashed towards the food storage unit which still had that ill-fitting door. He remembered that some damage had befallen that door at the time of construction. It wasn't important. There was no airlock associated with the storage unit. Nothing had been done about it. Arnold saw cats emerging from behind that bent door carrying food in their mouths as they ran off into the maelstrom.

Arnold played the video over and over again in disbelief before showing it to Molly. She, too, was unable to comprehend the phenomenon. Where had all those cats come from? Arnold called in the Wrights. The Wrights called in Nancy. Nancy called in Dusk. The footage was shown all over the settlement. There were many, many questions but no answers. The medics and other scientists in the party went into a conflab for several days until they finally felt able to explain everything. Their denouement took place as a round-table discussion which was broadcast throughout the settlement. They had one hundred percent attention.

They began by reminding people of the occasion when Mel and Trish's two white cats, Clarence and Unity, had disappeared via one of the pressure locks. Those two young cats were both pregnant at the time and, even after repeated searches, no trace of them could be found. It is our belief, the panel spokesperson said, that they had made a dash for the foot of the cliff where, as we later discovered, there are fissures leading down to underground liquid water and, even more to the point, an acceptable oxygen pressure. We further believe that they spent some time bathing in the warmth around one of the power plants in the cave near our settlement. As you know, those plants give off a fair amount of warmth and that would obviously have attracted those young cats. We presume further, that the power supply they chose to warm their toes on was the one we later discovered to have a small radiation leak. We believe that their unborn kittens were exposed to that radiation and that their DNA had been altered by the experience. One might have expected that such radiation damage would have caused their kittens to abort but it appears that they got away with it. But not entirely. We suggest that changes to their DNA resulted in probably several things, the most obvious being an ability to survive in a low-pressure atmosphere containing rather little oxygen; and a greatly reduced gestation period. In short, they breed like rabbits! Probably even faster. We recall that Arnold thought that Clarence and Unity were the offspring of Personage, who was black, you may remember, and of one of Mel and Trish's white cats, probably the one they imaginatively called Whitey. The fact that the children, grandchildren, and so on for goodness knows how many generations, are all white, grey, black or white streaked with black is therefore perfectly comprehensible. It is indeed fascinating to us that these cats are so hardy and lithe. There are obviously very many of them for their traces – admittedly, taken with time-lapse photography – to have been spotted from Earth.

There was a longish pause as the experts' audience took all this in. Arnold remembered that low-frequency noise he had heard in the cave after his accident some while back. He had been right! It was the sound of hundreds of happy cats, no doubt enjoying the smell of catnip everywhere. He must have been only metres away from them all!

And then came a shout from someone in the audience who Arnold didn't know.

'So the long and short of it is that we are surrounded by a thieving mob of feral cats!'

This produced some laughter, but rather more sounds of indignation. Then someone else called out, 'It's Arnold Forbutt and his bloody cats that are responsible for all these feral animals, robbing us of our vital food supplies.'

Molly was hurt beyond words. 'It wasn't deliberate,' she called out, 'You all loved the cats when they performed for us on the journey out here!'

Arnold went white and totally quiet. Then he said to Molly, for he had no intention of answering those calls directly, 'Here we go again, Molly. What are we supposed to do? Call the RSPCA? Look what happened last time. We can't go through all that again. In any case, we don't have Liz and Henry here.'

So flimsy and superficial was the over-lying dermis of civilization and civility of that society, so fickle were the protestations of fellowship and camaraderie, that almost before he had got the words out of his mouth, two of their fellow-settlers came up to Arnold to abuse him face-to-face.

'Bloody feral cats,' they shouted into his face, 'You started this. You've gotta solve it.'

'What do you want me to do?' Arnold yelled back, 'Chase them up one by one?'

'That's your problem,' another brute yelled in his face, 'You do something.'

Molly began to cry, which made Arnold lash out at his tormentors. Of course, they fought back, and Arnold found himself fighting off dozens of angry men – and even some women – until two of them held his arms and began punching him non-stop.

'Molly, Molly,' Arnold cried out, 'I didn't mean this to happen. I'm sorry. It's just that I loved those cats. I still do!'

At that, someone gave Arnold such a heavy punch that he yelled out uncontrollably, 'Molly, Molly…'

13

'Molly, Molly...' Arnold shouted. He was being shaken by his shoulder, more and more violently.

'Wake up, luv,' Molly was calling gently to him, 'Wake up. You're having a nightmare.

It was dark in their bedroom.

Their bedroom back in Australia. How had they got back? What had Dusk done?

'Calm yourself, my love,' Molly was saying, 'Whatever have you been dreaming of?'

'What about the cats?' asked Arnold, 'Are they all alright?' 'Yes, yes, they're fine, luv,' she replied, 'All four of them.'

'Four! What about the other four kittens? No nine!' Arnold replied, still quite frantic.

'What other four? Which nine?' Molly asked.

'WhiteOne, BrownOne, PaleGinger and BigWhiskers! And all the rest!' Arnold replied, with continuing alarm.

'What lovely names! But there are only four, luv. You have been dreaming.'

'Has Dusk sanctioned this?' Arnold continued. He was certainly not letting go easily.

'What had dusk got to do with anything?' Molly asked, 'It's the middle of the night, not dusk!'

'No: Noel Dusk!' Arnold insisted, but he was slowly beginning to realise that everything that had happened in the last couple of years, hadn't happened at all. He tried again: 'Have Andrew and Nina been to see them?' he asked next.

'What have Andrew and Nina got to do with the cats?' Molly asked. 'You mean there hasn't been a street party, we haven't been to Texas, we haven't been to Mars?'

'My goodness, you have had a dream. I hope you can remember it and write it all down,' Molly replied.

Arnold stopped talking and thought a bit. Then he remembered a lovely scene of eight cats holding onto each other's tails, forming a circle, and the circle slowly rotating. The scene slowly faded from view. He hugged Molly and Molly hugged him back.

***

In the morning, after taking their breakfast up to bed, Arnold said, 'Is it today that Liz and Henry bring the drop cage?' He had remembered that, in answer to their plea to complete the job of removing the last four cats, Henry had researched the matter and built a device called a drop cage. It comprised four sides and a top made of stout wire mesh attached to a wooden skirt. There was no bottom. When Henry brought it round later that morning, he explained how it was to be used. Arnold was to prop up the cage, which was quite heavy, and certainly too heavy for the cats to move, on a wooden stick, to the bottom of which was tied a long piece of strong string. Arnold was to place the cats' feeding bowls inside the cage and once they were all in there and gobbling away, he was to pull on the string so that the cage would fall over the cats.

'Hence drop cage,' Henry explained.

'It's going to be difficult to get them all in at one time, especially if I'm standing close to them,' Arnold complained. He didn't want to do this one little bit.

Henry explained: 'The string is very long so that you can run it inside the house and close the door, although not quite. Closed enough for you to disappear further indoors while still allowing the string to move when you pull the end.'

'Won't that heavy cage hurt their tails when it falls?' Arnold asked. He really didn't want to do this.

'No,' Henry replied, 'I've watched a video of a drop and, by instinct, the cats pull their tails in automatically,'

'Will our cats know that?' asked Arnold.

Arnold was less than convinced. It was agreed that Arnold should feed the cats within the cage for a few days so that the cats could get used to the setup and come in for their grub without pause. And so that's what they did for more than a week.

One day, Arnold phoned Liz to ask if it was convenient for him to do the deed tomorrow at breakfast time. Would that be convenient for their pick-up afterwards? Arnold simply couldn't bear to watch all that. It was all agreed.

At breakfast time next day, Arnold placed the bowls of food well back into the cage and watched as the cats trustingly came in to eat. He set the cage and retreated inside. Once he had got all four furry beasts within the cage and having placed spare pieces of wood under two corners so that the cage would not hit the deck flat, hence guaranteeing that their tails would not be caught, he retreated into the house and closed the glass door. The cats ate in confidence. Arnold pulled the string. There was a very loud crash, and four cats were trapped within the cage.

They were angry and frightened. Arnold couldn't blame them. He immediately phoned Liz: 'I've caught all four,' he said very quietly. Quietly because otherwise, he would have burst into tears.

'We'll be there straightaway,' Liz replied, hearing the angst in Arnold's voice.

Somehow, Arnold managed to finish making breakfast and took it upstairs to Molly. They would stay up there at least until Liz called to tell them that the cats had been removed. As he gave Molly her breakfast, Arnold completely lost it and cried like a baby. He couldn't speak. Molly leaped out of bed and put her arms round him. When he had calmed down a bit, he climbed into bed and they ate their breakfast in silence. Even the sounds from the TV were basically inaudible.

Liz called about three-quarters of an hour later. 'All done,' she said brightly, and tactfully left it at that.

Much later, Arnold learned from Henry that he and Liz had attached an ordinary carrying case to the back of the drop cage, opened a sluice gate between them, and all four cats had quietly accepted the situation and immediately walked through to be carried gently away to the RSPCA centre.

For the sake of accuracy and completeness, it should be recognised that the cat count was now zero.

Even weeks later, Arnold and Molly kept seeing visions of Snowflake, Blondie, Personage and Half Pint, and they would tear up.

'I do so miss them, luv,' Arnold said. 'So do I,' replied Molly.

They could barely see each other through fogs of tears.

NufSed